Murder in Watauga County

Other Books By Judi McGuire

A Guide to Becoming A Powerful Participant in the Political Process

Power, Poise, and True Prosperity: 21 Attributes of the 21st Century (A Study of Proverbs 31)

One Anothering: A Biblical Guide for Social Behavior

Bumps and Scrapes on the Road to Glory: Victorious Living at Any Age (with Mary Alice Kenley)

Murder in Blount County

Murder in Blount County: Cold Case Reopened

Murder in Blount County: Cliffhanger

Murder in St. Clair County: The Candidate

Woven Together: Created to be His Helpmate

Murder in Watauga County

Judi McGuire

Copyright © 2022 Judi McGuire

All rights reserved. No part of this publication may be used or reproduced by any means, graphic, electronic, or mechanical, including photocopying, recording, taping or by any information storage retrieval system without the written permission of the publisher except in the case of brief quotations embodied in critical articles and reviews.

ISBN: 9781717919229

First Printing 2023

Dedication

Since becoming an Alabama author, I have sought to dedicate each of my books to the person who best fits its theme. It is appropriate, therefore, that I dedicate this book to a friend who has helped me when I had writer's block and has always been eager to hear my latest chapter. His suggestions throughout the writing of this novel helped me to create a stronger story with unexpected turns. I value and respect his opinions and am grateful he enjoys Homer's adventures.

It is my honor to dedicate this novel to my friend,

Murk McKee

Contents

Acknowledgements

Chapter 1	Tomorrow Is Promised To No One	5
Chapter 2	Professor Yancey	29
Chapter 3	The Logbook	51
Chapter 4	Duke, Track!	75
Chapter 5	Gotcha, Homer	101
Chapter 6	Forensic Report	125
Chapter 7	The Investigation	145
Chapter 8	Investigative Detention	171
Chapter 9	To the Woodshed	193
Chapter 10	The Arrest	215
Chapter 11	Fabricating Evidence	233
Chapter 12	Get Rid of the Bugs	255
Chapter 13	Blue Wall of Silence	275
Chapter 14	Men in Black	295
Chapter 15	An Unexpected Suspect	317

Contents cont.

Chapter 16	Watchful Eyes	337
Chapter 17	Research Uncovers Clues	357
Chapter 18	The Engagement	379
Chapter 19	The Political Opponent	399
Chapter 20	The Withdrawal	419
Epilogue		445
About the Author		449
Judi McGuire – Alabama Author		451

Foreword

Murder mysteries are essentially spiritual in nature, focusing on the quest for truth and justice. The protagonist sets out to discover and expose the facts of what happened and bring wrongdoing to justice, and in this novel, he acts as an accomplice of God. In most murder mystery tales, the religious aspect of this mission is hidden, but in *Murder in Watauga County*, it spills onto the surface – like escaping blood – even as it is handled with utmost delicacy.

But this novel is no ordinary murder mystery. It resembles that genre; in many ways, it walks and talks like a murder mystery. But as the reader will soon discover, it does not fit that mold. To be sure, there's murder here, mystery, and a cop/detective protagonist, along with a plot momentum enough to keep the pages turning. However, all these elements are skewed in a way that makes for a more intensely personal work of art.

Take the page-turning. While the plot is certainly compelling, what pulls us, even more, is the setting, which is so minutely and masterfully observed and constantly rivets the reader's attention.

The deepest mystery here concerns the one character who is both most consequential and most invisible. The identity of this hidden protagonist I leave to the reader to explore.

I had the honor of discussing this story at the time my mother was composing it, and once a month, after a scrumptious dessert and some conversation, we would listen, rapt, as the latest installment of the new work unfolded. I was enthralled then, and I remain enthralled after several readings. When my mother asked me to write a foreword, I thought I'd just quickly skim the novel to refresh my mind. But after one page I knew I was hooked again, and I treated myself to re-reading every word.

This is the mark of first-rate literature: successive readings yield greater depth and increasing pleasure. I envy those who are about to embark on this journey for the first time.

Tanna McGuire

Preface

My name is Judi McGuire, and of the ten books I have written, this is my fifth fiction murder mystery novel to be published. The settings for the first four mysteries were in Alabama where my husband and I reside. This novel, however, takes place in Watauga County, North Carolina.

In my hometown, I am blessed to have friends in law enforcement. The Blount County Sheriff, the Hayden City Chief of Police, and the Oneonta Chief of Police are friends who are very accessible and always eager to provide me with reliable information which I am able to incorporate in my books. I do extensive research to ensure accuracy in my writing. For several months I have had the privilege of working with Oneonta City Detective Steven Adamson. He equipped me with behind-the-scenes techniques which helped me in presenting a true account of how a detective solves complex cases.

This book took over a year to write. It was challenging for several reasons. First, it was set in another state, requiring more research regarding laws, law enforcement procedures, and topographical features.

Second, this novel is the longest one I have written. I tried to stay at 2,500 words per chapter and nearly 60,000 words for the book.

The last challenge caused a slight delay in writing with the passing of my friend, Bobby Seals. When writing one of my books a few years ago, I realized that I was physically describing Bobby as Homer. After considerable thought, I have decided to continue to use Homer as the main character in my books.

As Homer would say, "Take your own sweet time, and enjoy *Murder in Watauga County*." Perhaps you'll be able to figure out *whodunit* before it's revealed to you.

Judi McGuire

Acknowledgements

Authoring this novel was more difficult than I thought and more rewarding than I could have ever imagined. Having an idea and turning it into a book is as hard as it sounds. The experience is both internally challenging and gratifying. I especially want to thank individuals who helped make this happen. My humble thanks to the Lord for His love, and for His mercy in allowing me to finish this, my tenth book.

I mostly want to thank my beloved husband, **Tim McGuire.** I have so much to thank you for – for being such a smart, insightful first editor who helped me unravel so many problems and story lines, for all those brain-storming sessions when I needed to elaborate more, for all those late-night, last-minute read-throughs, for your insistence that the book was good. You have extraordinary intelligence, humor, and lovingkindness. I am still amazed that you have co-authored my life. Thank you for sometimes just offering me a song and a kiss at the end of the day. I would never have come so far without you by my side.

To my book designer, **Tanna McGuire.** I chose Tanna as the cover designer for two reasons. First, she recognized that the purpose of a book cover is more than merely decoration. It is to attract potential readers to the book by giving just a glimpse of it. Tanna is a gifted artist who understands that a compelling visual can help make a connection with the reader without them even needing to turn the first page. The second reason I chose Tanna is because she is my talented, beloved daughter.

To my editor, **Becky Smith.** Most editors are looking for fame or glory, but acquiring recognition is not Becky's goal. She is not employed by a renowned publishing company, yet she is the best editor I have ever had. Even though she was carrying enormous personal burdens, she fulfilled her commitment to edit this novel for one reason, to lay down her life for a friend. Thank you, Becky, for loving me and for your tireless efforts to perfect this novel.

A special thanks to **Investigator Corporal Steven Adamson** of the Oneonta Police Department for answering my endless list of questions on how a detective solves a case. You shared information which helped enhance the story with accurate investigative procedures. I sincerely thank you for your help.

To my sister-in-law, **Sybil Hendricks,** and to my friends **Murk McKee, Scherrlinda Higginbothan,** and **David and Leah Simmons** for their willingness to listen to drafts before I submitted the transcript to the editor.

Chapter One
Tomorrow is Promised to No One

It was not a sweltering day, but his anxiety caused him to keep the air-conditioning on high as he drove to Spartanburg, South Carolina, a city just across the North Carolina state line. He knew he was getting close when all the billboards began to point to the Spartanburg Convention Center.

South Carolina's gun control laws were among the least restrictive in the nation, which was what he needed — a place to buy a gun that was difficult to be traced. Many gun transfers at a gun show in South Carolina did not require background checks, standard legal protocol, or permits to buy and own firearms, including rifles, shotguns, and handguns.

When he reached the entrance to the convention center, a member of the National Rifle Association offered him free access with a six-month membership. Because he wanted to avoid a paper trail regarding information on himself, he chose to pay the entrance fee.

He was not expecting to see such a large convention center when he stepped inside! The 50,000 square foot building was filled with booths designed to sell firearms. He guesstimated at least eighty or more vendors, in addition to sellers walking down each aisle carrying guns to be sold on the spot. The sound of the cocking of firearms bounced off the metal ceiling and the noise was compounded by the loud chatter from eager buyers bartering for the right price.

People who wanted to sell guns without accountability to the government started following him, asking if he wanted to buy a firearm cheap. It reminded him of a trip he once made to Central America, where people wanted him to buy cheaply made souvenirs, only this time, what he wanted was not cheap.

Out of sheer frustration and annoyance, he finally turned around and stopped. He asked one of the persistent guys who had been following him, "Do you have a Colt .22 caliber revolver?"

The smiling man replied, "As a matter of fact, I have one right here inside my jacket." Before looking in his jacket, the man put on a pair of rubber gloves. He unzipped his jacket and located the handgun which was attached to the inside of his jacket with Velcro. After detaching the gun, he gently handed it to him.

The buyer also had slipped on a pair of gloves. "I he asked.

After taking his gun back from him, the salesman said, "I'll be right back," then disappeared into the crowd.

A few minutes later, he felt a tap on his shoulder.

The salesman said, "This silencer is made for the Colt .22 caliber revolver. If you are ready to make a purchase, then we can close this deal."

"Not until you agree to my conditions," the man said.

The salesman had a puzzled look on his face. "What are your conditions?" he reluctantly asked.

"I don't want to register the gun or the silencer," he said.

The salesman assured the man that his gun did not have to be registered in South Carolina.

"Sir, silencers are required by law in our state to be registered. If you want to avoid that process, then you need to talk to the man dressed in camo. He is standing next to the vending machines. But before we do that, if you intend to purchase the gun and silencer, then let's close that deal first," the salesman insisted.

"How much for the gun and the silencer?" he asked in a low voice. He could tell the guy was anxious to make a sale, but nervous about selling him an illegal silencer.

"How does $800 for everything sound?"

"Would you take $700?" he asked.

"No, but you can have them for $750."

"Deal," he said. He put his purchase in the Convention Center tote bag given to him when he entered the gun show.

He removed his gloves before reaching into his pocket. He pulled out a wad of money and counted out $750 in fifties.

The salesman tilted his head in the direction of the man in camo. He and the buyer shook hands and then the salesman left.

The buyer told the man beside the vending machines his intent to not register the silencer.

"Not a problem," the man said.

He led the buyer to a backroom and within minutes there was no trace of the silencer ever being purchased. They shook hands and the required fee was paid.

As he made his way through the crowd to the exit, he listened to an upbeat song by a bluegrass group on stage called the Pine Mountain Possum Pickers from Blount County, Alabama. He smiled with satisfaction.

As he was leaving Spartanburg on Hwy 26, he noticed a gun shop. He had neglected to buy ammunition at the Convention Center, so he decided to stop. He paid in cash. When he got back in the truck, he looked on the passenger seat at the gun and silencer and said, "Tomorrow is promised to no one."

The following week, he took two days off work and drove to Kentucky for the sole purpose of trying out his new gun at a public firing range.

He was careful to always wear gloves when holding the gun or silencer. He was trained to know that wearing gloves was beneficial if you are just getting used to handling a new gun.

The tote bag was on the passenger seat of his truck. When he reached in the bag to get the pistol, he saw the slip of paper the gun seller had given him. His eyes focused on this one sentence, "You can't determine a great deal about your gun's accuracy unless you shoot a lot of rounds. Evaluating guns is a mix of hard science and firing the weapon to simulate the gun being used in its intended role." He laughed at the testing instructions, tucked the gun in his coat pocket, and walked towards the firing range.

He did not want anyone to know he had received safety and firing instructions years ago, so he decided to pretend he was a novice and take the course offered at the range.

Mike Allison was the course instructor. The very first things that Mike brought up were four rules he said if strictly followed, would help everyone to have a safe and enjoyable time unloading a few rounds.

"First, always treat every firearm as if it were loaded—no ifs, ands, or buts. Even if you know the gun is unloaded, manage it as if it were loaded.

"Second, always keep the firearm pointed in a safe direction, a direction where a careless discharge would cause minimum property damage and zero physical injury," Mike said. He added that even the most experienced gun handlers break this rule occasionally.

"Next," Mike added, "always keep your trigger finger off the trigger and outside the trigger guard until you have made a conscious decision to fire your weapon.

"And last," Mike said in conclusion, "Always be sure of your target, backstop, and beyond. You want to be aware of what is in your line of fire. At a professional gun range this shouldn't be a concern. We make sure people and property stay out of the path of the firing guns."

The instructor then talked about gripping a handgun, assuming the extended shooting position, and aiming a firearm.

Finally, it was time to evaluate the newly purchased gun. He could only fire for an hour because that was the limit for using the range when other people waited. Since he was a marksman, the little time he spent on the firing range to evaluate his new gun was sufficient.

When he got into his truck, he saw the paperwork he read earlier laying on the seat, and said to himself, "Let's see, oh, here it is." He read again where it said, "Fire the weapon to simulate the gun being used in its intended role." Still laughing, he said, "As soon as I can, as soon as I can."

The following day, he put a shovel in the trunk of his rental car and drove down the road towards Wilbur Lake. He constantly observed his surroundings to be careful he wasn't being followed or noticed. With the assumption that he was not seen, he parked his car, got out at a location he considered to be ideal and walked into the woods. Within a few feet, he found a level area out of sight from the road. It seemed like the right spot so he started digging. When he finished, he drove further down the road until he reached the lake, where he rinsed the shovel and left.

Later that afternoon, he drove to the church. Since the pastor lived across the street from the church, he glanced towards Pastor White's house. He wanted to make certain that he was not home. The pastor's car was not parked at his house.

He proceeded to the rear of the building and noticed only one car parked near the entrance. He parked his car and went straight to the church secretary's office.

Stephanie heard a sound at the door to her office that startled her. When she looked over her shoulder, she was frightened by the sight of a man wearing latex gloves, a face mask, shoe coverings, and a head covering.

She recognized his voice when he asked, "Why are you going to do this to me, Stephanie?"

"Because you deserve it for being deceitful. Why are you dressed like that?" Stephanie asked. She stood, knocking over her Diet Dr. Pepper onto the church newsletter she had just printed. Ignoring the mess she made, she looked at him with fear in her eyes.

He did not answer her.

She felt a strong blow to the back of her neck and immediately fell into his arms, unconscious.

He knew he had to act quickly. He placed her limp body inside a large, doubled leaf bag and dragged her lifeless body to the car. He carefully avoided the surveillance cameras installed in the church and outside the entrance. He used all precautions not to be recognized.

After he got to the car, he placed her body in the back seat. He drove slowly towards Wilbur Lake Road which was surrounded by a beautiful forest. The road ended at Wilbur Lake.

In the meantime, back at the church, a man stepped out of the supply closet. He was frightened. He cautiously looked around to see if it was safe to leave the building without being seen. No one was in the church, so he briskly walked to the back door and exited the building. He carefully checked his surroundings then hurriedly crossed the church yard to his house next door.

When the assailant reached the spot where he had dug a pit, he stopped the car, picked up the leaf bag containing Stephanie's body, and carried her to the burial pit.

He wanted to follow his well-thought-out plan, so once he lowered her into the burying place, he opened the leaf bag slightly. He took aim at her head and pulled the trigger, then closed the leaf bag and buried her. When he finished, he made the area as natural-looking as possible, got back in the car, and drove to the lake where he placed the shovel in a weighted plastic bag and sat at a picnic table until he was certain no one was watching. He flung the bag as far as he could, then watched it slowly sink into the deepest portion of the lake.

He returned to his car, then maneuvered through heavy traffic enroute to the hospital. He drove around back and parked close to the dumpsters and waited. Ten minutes later, he got out of the car and walked to the middle dumpster where he threw in a small bag containing his face mask, latex gloves, shoe coverings, and head covering.

After surveying his surroundings, he was confident no one saw him, so he drove away. The gun and silencer were not registered, so he kept them.

Stephanie's husband, Matthew, called his wife's cell phone, but his call went straight to voicemail. He then called the church office. Again, there was no answer.

Stephanie was the church secretary and it was common for her to get deeply involved in her work. However, she always looked forward to their Thursday night date at the Dan'l Boone Restaurant. Even if she was busy, she would always answer Matthew's calls.

Matthew was beginning to be worried and decided it would be wise to go to the church and check on his wife. He drove to the rear of the church and parked. He was truly relieved to see her car. Matthew hurried to the back door and found it unlocked. He had constantly reminded Stephanie to keep the church locked when she was alone.

He rushed down the hallway to the church office. The door was open, but Stephanie was not there. Her computer was on, and her purse looked as though it had been shoved across the floor. There was a spilled Diet Dr. Pepper all over her desk and the floor. "Stephanie! Stephanie!" He shouted as he walked towards the women's restroom. He knocked on the door before opening it.

"Stephanie, are you here?" There was no answer. He continued his search, but his wife was nowhere in the building. He went back to his wife's office, and because he wasn't thinking clearly. He wanted to help but was not sure what to do. He noticed the trashcan was practically full, so on an impulse, he picked it up, and he emptied it outside in the dumpster.

He went back inside, put the trashcan back in her office, and seeing his wife's purse, he wondered why it had apparently been slid across the floor. He picked it up and opened it. When he saw his wife's rings and wallet inside, he knew he needed to protect them, so he took the purse outside and put it in his car. Matthew was breathing hard and getting more and more anxious and scared for his beloved wife.

Once inside the building, he decided to call the pastor. The distraught husband realized in his haste he had left his cell phone in his car. He went straight to the pastor's office and called from there, getting no answer. He called several times until finally, Pastor White answered.

"Hello, this is Pastor Henry."

"Henry, this is Matthew. Have you seen or heard from Stephanie?" When he got a negative answer, he told the pastor his concern for her safety.

"Matthew, I'll be right there." The pastor lived across the street from the church, so he arrived in less than five minutes. Matthew met him at the back door and suggested they talk in the pastor's office.

"Henry, I'm scared. Stephanie doesn't do things like this. I searched the entire church and didn't find her. She wasn't in her office. Her computer was on, and there was a spilled drink on her desk and the floor. All of her belongings were still there. I saw her purse and for safety reasons, I put it in my car to take home."

"It probably will be safe there, but we need to let the police know where it is, don't you think?" asked Pastor White.

"I don't know. Her purse isn't important, but she is," responded Matthew.

"As you know, Matthew, Sheriff Allan Reed is a member of this church. I'm not trying to alarm you, but I think we should call him," said the pastor. "Don't you agree? I'm sure she didn't leave with a girlfriend or someone else, because not only is she a very responsible person, but she loves you very much, and she would have let you know her plans."

The pastor could see the tears in Matthew's eyes, so he said, "Matthew, let's pray for Stephanie's safety and for the Lord to give you peace. They paused, bowed their heads, and the pastor prayed.

"Thanks, Henry. Who else should I call? The Boone Chief of Police? 911?"

"I think since we suspect foul play, we need to call the chief and the sheriff," answered Henry. "I have their cell phone numbers right here on my desk," he said as he placed the first call.

"Allan? Pastor Henry White. How are you?"

"Okay, I guess. How can I help you?" Allan asked.

Henry explained the situation and told the sheriff that he and Matthew were concerned for Stephanie's safety.

"Are you at the church now?"

"Yes. We're in my office."

"I'm going to send Steven Adamson, my Chief Deputy Sheriff, there right away and let him take all the information we need to start investigating her disappearance. I won't be able to come because I'm in charge of a meeting that starts in a few minutes. I hope you understand," said the sheriff.

"Certainly, we'll be on the lookout for your deputy," Pastor White said.

"Okay, Matthew, let's call Chief Daniel Cornelius."

After the call, Matthew broke down crying in the pastor's office while they waited for law enforcement. Matthew told Henry, "This is my worst nightmare. We have got to find her!"

Deputy Adamson arrived about fifteen minutes later, followed by a policeman. They told Matthew that they would do everything possible to find his wife. Deputy Adamson started the questioning. " I need your full name, address, and phone number.

"Mr. Wright, the first thing I want to do is check Watauga Medical Center and the county jail. That's routine, Mr. Wright. Now I need information regarding your wife, including birth date, age, physical description, and most importantly, any medical information. Where was your wife before she disappeared?" asked Deputy Adamson.

Matthew told the deputy that Stephanie was the church secretary. "I went to her office to see if she was still working. She wasn't there, but her office was in disarray. It appeared to me that she left in a hurry."

Chapter Two
Professor Yancey

Matthew led the two law enforcement officers to Stephanie's office. Deputy Adamson, who was an investigator, observed that her computer was turned on and there was a spilled drink on her desk and the floor. Deputy Adamson photographed the room with his cell phone camera and carefully documented his interview with Matthew.

"We intend to secure this room and no one is to enter. This is extremely important, as there may be evidence we need to uncover. We cannot take a chance that potential evidence is compromised. Do you understand? Not only do we intend to cordon off this office but the hallways to the exits as well.

"Mr. Wright, it would be helpful if you would provide us with a few names and phone numbers of her closest friends. We also need her cell phone number, e-mail address, password, and social networking information.

"We're sure all of this must be overwhelming for you, Mr. Wright. Perhaps it will be reassuring that when an adult has been reported missing to police, their name and personal information are entered into a nationwide database, which will assist other law enforcement agencies in helping us find her.

"However, Mr. Wright, since being a missing person is not a crime, we are given a minimal role while conducting these investigations. Generally, all people have a right to be left alone, and police intrusion into their lives must be minimal. Until further investigation, we cannot assume there has been foul play; however, we are going to assign additional resources, including local, state, and federal agencies, if foul play is determined. We want to assure you, Mr. Wright, that we will do whatever possible to find your missing wife," said Boone Police Officer Gene Hinkle.

Meanwhile, Homer called his team together at the bunkhouse. Homer Yancey is a humble man from Alabama who rose to stardom after solving several complex murder cases. Mr. Yancey is president of the Yancey Investigative Services and is worth $5.2 million.

"Mornin,' y'all. I done got me a letter from reckon they want me to talk to their Criminal Justice class. Says here," he said as he read from the letter. "It's part of the Department of Government and Justice Studies. They want me to tell 'em about how we do our investigatin' and tell 'em about some cases we figgered out. I reckon it looks like word's gittin' out that we find out whodunit.

"Y'all keep tellin' me I'm the number one detective and the boss man, but y'all know that we're a team. If my durn memory serves me well, and last time I checked, it does," Homer said with a grin. "Y'all told me that where I go, you go. So, we're going to Boone, North Carolina, next week!

"Before I let y'all know the other reason we're going thar, I'm gonna tell ya about the place we're going to. I got that thar computer thingamajig y'all done got me fer Christmas and I learnt all about the place," Homer paused because Brayden wished to say something, which irritated Homer. "What's up, Brayden? If ye got somethang to say, just say it."

"Homer, I'm proud of you for being a techie." Everyone laughed but Homer.

"Anyhow, Boone is a little ole town in Watauga County, North Carolina. It's up thar in the top western part of the Blue Ridge Mountains. This here town is whar the campus of Appalachian State University sits and whar Franklin Graham has his headquarters for his Samaritan's Purse Ministry.

"Guess who the town is named fer, Brayden?" Homer asked, smiling.

"Is it Daniel Boone?"

"Yep." Homer grinned, then said, "Y'all gonna like this here part. The reason I want y'all to come with me is," Homer stopped to shuffle papers, then after clearing his throat to add drama, he said, "Drum roll, please, guys." The guys accommodated his request.

Finally, Homer read from what he printed off the internet, "Towering peaks, fly fishing, clear mountain streams, and year-round scenery are the hallmarks of the Watauga River Basin." He stopped long enough for that to sink in. "We're goin' on a fishing trip and have some fun fer a change!!" The team went wild with excitement!!

"Tell us more Homer!"

"What kind of fish, Homer?"

"Can we go canoeing?"

"Kayaking?"

"Whitewater rafting?"

Everyone spoke at once.

"Brayden, do you mind settin' this trip up fer us? I'd like fer us all to stay in one big cabin in Boone. Rite cheer is the letter from the University tellin' me what they want me to tell 'em students about what we've done and how we solve our cases. Please thank 'em fer inviting me and say that I eagerly accept. Also, when settin' thangs up fer us, be sure and add one more week fer our vacation. Duke and I'll stay in one room in the cabin. You figger out the rest," Homer said, grinning. He was enormously proud of his team and for this opportunity to relax with them.

"One more thang, guys. I have kin folks up thar, so make me proud. By the way, Tom, what is the son of my first cousin called?" asked Homer.

"He is your first cousin once removed. Just introduce him as your cousin."

"His name is Matthew Wright, and I want ye to meet him when we git to Boone. His wife disappeared about six weeks ago, and he said the investigation is now just a cold case. She either done walked out on him, or there's foul play and lousy detective work."

"Sounds like you had a couple of reasons for accepting the University's invitation," replied Tom.

A week later, the announcement Homer was waiting on came from the flight attendant. "Ladies and gentlemen, we have just been cleared to land at the Tri-Cities Regional Airport. Please make sure your seat belt is securely fastened. Thank you."

After the touchdown, the flight attendant made one last announcement after turning off the active runway and taxiing to the gate.

"Ladies and gentlemen, welcome to Tri-Cities Regional Airport. Local time is 12:14 p.m. Eastern Daylight Time and the temperature is 81 degrees."

"Man, am I glad to git off that dad burn plane. Hey, Brayden, let's take the train home," laughed Homer. "Hey, why is that man holding a sign with my name on it?" Tom approached the man and introduced Homer. "Homer, this man will be taking us to our cabin in Boone."

Homer replied, "Let's skedaddle!"

It was forty-five miles from the airport to the cabin on the Watauga River. Homer and his dog, Duke, were in one room, and Tom Lynch, Tyler Frye, Brayden Davis and Zach and Victoria Thomas, all had their own rooms.

Zach and Victoria volunteered to drive to North Carolina and bring Duke. They knew Homer would be upset if Duke had to fly with the luggage under the plane, so they rented a car and drove to North Carolina with Duke in the back seat. When the team got to the cabin, Zach and

Victoria were already settled into their room and had even bought groceries for the next several meals.

The rest of the day was fun and relaxing. Two team members wanted to fish and Homer napped while Zach and Victoria went canoeing. After a brief rest, Homer stayed in his room and reviewed his speech for the next morning's Criminal Justice class.

After a good night's sleep, the team was picked up by a staff member from the University. Right on cue, they entered the classroom dressed in dark business suits. Tom Lynch entered first, followed by Tyler, Zach, and Brayden, and trailing behind came Homer Yancey dressed in jeans, an untucked shirt, a jacket, and a matching ball cap. The professor grinned when he saw Homer. Even though his team members were wearing suits and all the students and the professor were wearing suits, Homer was not intimidated. In fact, he didn't even apologize for his appearance.

Turning his attention to the class, the instructor said, "This is the renowned investigative team from Alabama, Yancey Investigative Services. Gentlemen, please be seated. Now, allow me to introduce Homer Yancey."

The professor briefly told the class about how Homer became a detective, then said, "You didn't come to hear me talk today," laughed the professor. "Class please welcome Mr. Homer Yancey. Mr. Yancey?" The students applauded but looked puzzled as Homer took the podium, not only because of his appearance, but mainly because of his broken English.

Homer began by saying, "Today I'm responsible fer what I say, not what ye understand. I believe that the most important thang ye gotta remember 'bout what I say today is this — The Golden Rule with Yancey Investigative Services is, 'Don't touch, change, or move any thang at the crime scene unless it is well marked, measured, sketched, or photographed.' I'm gonna tell ye why this here is important in a little bit, but first, I want y'all to meet the Yancey team.

"Tom, stand up. Tom Lynch used to be a Criminal Justice professor at Jacksonville State University in Jacksonville, Alabama until I got him to go to work with us. He is my right-hand man and I keep him busy as a cat on a hot tin roof.

"Tyler, stand up. Next is Tyler Frye, who majored in Criminal Justice at JSU. He was in Tom's classes at the University and I reckon he was his brightest student. He's got a good eye for finding evidence.

PROFESSOR YANCEY

"Next is Zach Thomas." Homer motioned for Zach to stand up. "Zach and Tom are kinfolks. Zack is Tom's nephew and is the lawyer on our team. Trust me, he knows the law and makes sure we do, too.

"Next is Brayden Davis." Homer motioned for Brayden to stand up. "He's one of our detectives and knows the right thangs to ask of witnesses and possible suspects, and he knows what he's doing and takes care of the little thangs. Thanks, guys, you can sit back down," Homer said grinning with pride.

"You're probably taking this class 'cause you're wantin' to be an investigator. Let me tell ye how I started doing this job." He briefly gave examples of the cases he was involved with and was able to solve. "Some cases," he said, "I told 'em I'd help 'cause I wanted to, and some I was asked to solve 'cause it was a cold case."

Homer then asked, "Do ye have an investigative mind? Investigators like to solve problems. Wherever they're at, they git information and chew on it awhile before deciding what to do next.

"Being a good detective takes a combination of natural abilities and learned skills. I wanna suggest some skills you need to learn. First, you need to be able to notice things others may not see and then connect the dots.

"Do you have a good memory? You need one so you can 'member clues and conversations then organize that information.

"If the professor talks about interviews and interrogation skills, listen to what he has to say. You have to learn to ask the right questions, watch body language and what is said. Many of the skills you need in order to be good detectives you will learn in this class, but some of you already have natural abilities."

Homer kept the students captivated with his keen understanding of the investigative process and kept them laughing with his one-liners.

Homer glanced at his watch. "You're gittin' tired because I can tell you're gittin' short on ears and I'm probably gittin' long on mouth." Everyone laughed. Homer wished the students success in their studies and left the room. Once outside, his teammates showed him their enthusiastic approval by patting him on the back or hugging him.

"Homer, we need to get you on the speaker's circuit. You were terrific!" Tom said as he shook Homer's hand.

"Thanks, guys. Hey, Brayden, how 'bout rentin' us a car so we can go where we want to when we want to? We'll be in the student center drinking a hot cup of java," Homer said. He motioned for Brayden to step aside for a moment. "I know you ain't our secretary, but I wanta thank ye fer how you organize stuff and are good 'bout settin' things up fer us. Between us, you'll be gittin' a bonus check for this."

"Thanks, Homer!"

While drinking their coffee, Homer told the team about his cousin, Matthew, and all about his wife's disappearance. "He lives here in Boone, and I called him last night. He done told me 'bout when his wife went missin' and how the investigation's been slow as molasses. I want to tell y'all what he done told me 'bout the case over supper at the cabin."

As they ate a light meal that evening, Homer told how his cousin was worried when his wife did not show up for their weekly date night.

"Matthew said he went to the church where she worked to check on her. Her car was there, but Stephanie wasn't. He said the deputy sheriff and a Boone cop came to the church and took some information about Stephanie from him. Everyone finally agreed that she was taken against her will. That's when they started investigatin.'

"The local sheriff, Allan Reed, is a member of Matthew's church and is head of the investigation. Not only is Stephanie still missing, but there ain't no good leads in the case.

"Matthew done asked me if we'd like to take over the case. I'd guess Sheriff Reed would be glad to hand it off 'cause he's probably got a bunch of crime in a county the size of Watauga. If ye don't mind staying here fer a while in this purdy part of the country, I reckon we can work and play. What do ye say?" Homer paused for a reaction.

Smiling, they all nodded affirmatively.

"Okay, thanks. I'll call Matthew tonight and tell him we're all in. I'll see if he'll set up a meetin' fer us with the sheriff. I'll ask Matthew to go with us." Homer yawned and told everybody that it had been a long day and that he was plum tuckered out. "I want y'all to rise and shine in the morning so we can chow down together 'round 7:00 a.m. Don't forget we are in a different time zone now. Morning comes earlier here. 7:00 o'clock here is 6:00 o'clock Alabama time. This here is jest a reminder to set your watches while we're here. I'm going to bed now. Night, y'all." Homer took Duke for a short walk before heading to his room.

Before he went to sleep, Homer decided to call Matthew. He answered on the third ring. "Matthew, it's Homer. The team said they was sorry 'bout your wife and would shore nuff be happy to lend a hand and help find her."

"That's great, Homer. Thanks."

"Can ye set up a meetin' fer us with the sheriff? We'd like to meet him and find out what he's learnt 'bout what happened to Stephanie. I like fer ye to go with us. Can you do that?"

"You bet. I'll call Allan in the morning and see if he's available sometime tomorrow. I also want him to know that I hired Yancey Investigative Services and that I would like him to meet the team. I'll let you know what he says. Thanks so much, Homer. I'm glad you're here."

The following day everyone was seated at the kitchen table drinking coffee when Homer walked in.

"We have bagels and cream cheese, egg, cheese, and Canadian bacon on an English muffin, or large blueberry muffins. Which do you prefer?" asked Victoria.

"No bagel. My doc won't let me have one. But the blueberry muffin shore smells good. Thanks, Victoria," Homer said and kissed her on the cheek.

"Homer, have you seen that sailboat anchored in the river in front of our cabin? It must be 30-feet long! Have you ever been sailing, Homer?" asked Tyler.

"Yeah. It ain't hard to learn. That sailboat is only twenty-six feet. I rented it, and my cousin Matthew said he'd be mighty proud to be our 'Captain.' He done said he'd teach y'all how to sail it."

"You never cease to amaze me, Homer. Thanks. Can we go now?" asked Tyler.

"No, but don't pitch no duck fit. We gotta git some work done first. Maybe later today we can sail up this purdy river. Also, I know you young folks want to do stuff other than just sailing. I'm thankin' we need to go git fishin' licenses fer everybody, git a boatin' license, and git some food. We gotta rent kayaks, canoes, and fishin' poles. Life preservers are already on the boat. I told ye we're here fer some fun, too."

Homer sat at the table, drank his coffee, and slowly ate his muffin. "I talked to Matthew this morning, and we gotta meetin' with the sheriff at 10:30 a.m. today. Tom, I'd like fer ye to go with Matthew and me. Zach, do ye and

Victoria mind gitting' the stuff we'll need to have fun on this river? Watauga means Beautiful River. It is, don't ye think?"

"Yes, it is, and we gladly accept that assignment!" responded Zach.

Chapter 3
The Logbook

When Matthew arrived at the cabin, he was introduced to everyone. After small talk, he, Tom, and Homer left to meet with Sheriff Reed.

When the men arrived at the Watauga Sheriff's Department, they were greeted by Heather, Sheriff Reed's secretary. She immediately escorted them to the sheriff's office.

"Hello, Mr. Yancey. I knew you were in town. Nice to have famous people come for a visit. Please have a seat. To what do I owe this honor?"

"Sheriff, I want to introduce you to my cousin, Homer. As you know, he's a private detective. Also, this is Tom Lynch who is also a detective and works with Homer. We're here today because I wanted you to know that I have hired Yancey Investigative Services to coordinate the search for my wife," explained Matthew.

"That's wonderful, Mr. Yancey. With a county this large, I'm pulled in all directions putting out fires. I welcome your help in finding Mrs. Wright. Thank you. Now, how can I help you?" asked the sheriff as he leaned back in his chair and folded his arms behind his head.

"We'd like to git a copy of your file on Stephanie, so we won't have to do the same stuff that's you've done already. My cousin's heart is broke, and we want to help him find out what happened on that terrible day that she disappeared. She might have done walked away or maybe somethang bad done happened to her," Homer told Sheriff Reed.

THE LOGBOOK

"Absolutely," the sheriff responded. "I wish I got paid by the pile," he said as he laughed and swept across the top of his desk with his hand. "Let me get Heather to provide you with a copy of Mrs. Wright's file." He pressed the button on his intercom and gave instructions to his secretary.

A few minutes later, Heather entered the room and handed a file to Sheriff Reed. The sheriff thanked her and then handed the file to Homer. Homer took the copy and flipped through the pages. He asked for clarification on two things, then handed the file to Tom.

"Sheriff, Tom was a professor of Criminal Justice at Jacksonville State University in Alabama before joining our team. He taught me the rite way to do investigatin'. No doubt he's the most valuable one on our team.

Sir, I'd like to personally thank ye and your deputies fer all ye folks have done fer my cousin. As you know, he's pretty messed up since his wife disappeared without a trace. I'm sure we'll keep needin' your hep with this case.

"Well, we'd like to come back and talk with ye again if that's okay. Here's my card with my number if ye need me for any thang."

"Thank you for your time, and it was nice to meet you," said Tom as they stood to leave.

Once they were in the car, Tom said, "Homer that was brilliant for you to ask the sheriff for his file on the investigation. I'm glad we're taking the file home because we need to know every detail of it and see what has been uncovered and if there is anything the sheriff might have missed."

THE LOGBOOK

"Probably when the investigation started, the sheriff had his deputies' tape off Stephanie's office to limit access. Now that it's our case, I'd like fer us to go to the church to see where she worked. How 'bout it, Matthew? Can we go thar now?" Homer asked.

"Sure. I guess it has been a while since you have been there, huh, Homer?" asked Matthew.

"When did you go there?" asked Tom.

"I was baptized in that thar church years ago," answered Homer. "I wonder if it still looks the same."

"There have been some changes in the last one hundred years," remarked Matthew with a grin.

"Be afraid, be very afraid, young man!" Homer said.

They arrived at the Hickory Grove Baptist Church fifteen minutes later. Matthew parked in the back, turned the engine off, and was quiet for a moment.

"Are you alright, Matthew?" asked Tom.

"I parked in this spot when I checked on Stephanie the night she disappeared. I'm okay. Let's go inside. I see Pastor Henry's car, and I'd like for you to meet him."

The pastor was in his office. Matthew knocked before entering, so they wouldn't startle him. Matthew introduced Homer and Tom and told the pastor about hiring his cousin's firm to take over the investigation of Stephanie's mysterious disappearance. The pastor was thrilled to hear the news and told Tom and Homer that he'd be praying for them.

THE LOGBOOK

Like most pastors, he was outgoing and talkative, but Homer politely stood and told him they had a job to do today but hoped to talk again soon.

"Pastor, since I have keys to the church, do you mind if I come with these men and let them in while they investigate Stephanie's disappearance?" asked Matthew.

The pastor grinned, "I'd want you to do that, Matthew, but there is no need for you to go to all that trouble. I have an extra set of keys here in my desk." He fumbled around in his messy desk drawer until he found a set of keys, then handed them to Homer.

"Mr. Yancey, I'm eager to help in any way I can. Not only was Stephanie a member of this church, but she was also the church secretary. If you need me for any reason, you can find me here in my office every morning.

Lord bless you, gentlemen. See you, Matthew." The men shook hands with the pastor and left.

When they walked out of the pastor's office, Homer slapped his forehead and said, "I'm sorry, Matthew. Can we see Stephanie's office tomorrow? I done made a promise to everybody this morning while we were eatin' breakfast that I just remembered. I promised them that after we met with the sheriff, we'd have fun on the river.

"Matthew, I know how I'd be if I walked into Stephanie's office rite now and started looking around. It'd be nigh suppertime before I knew it. Please, can we come back here first thang in the morning, say around eight?"

"I understand, cousin. You have a set of keys to the church, but this one is to Stephanie's office," he said as he handed Homer his wife's office key. "I must work tomorrow. You have my cell phone number if you need me for any reason. Also, I know I promised your team a tour of the Watauga River on that fancy sailboat you rented, so let's get back to your cabin and get everyone on board!"

"Thanks, Matthew. Would it be all right to bring my dog, Duke, tomorrow? He graduated from his training at the Canine Detection Research Institute at Auburn University. He got himself a diploma and everythang. He's now certified to do police work. Duke's officially a part of our team."

"That's terrific, Homer. Of course, he can come with you. I'd like to know more about his training!"

"Maybe later, but for now, let's take us a ride on that sailboat!"

For the rest of the day, the team enjoyed their tour of the Watauga River. The Watauga River Basin surrounded by mountain peaks was the area the group enjoyed the most. This area was where they saw a lot of people fly fishing.

They only toured the North Carolina portion of the Watauga River Basin, which included the headwaters and tributaries of the Watauga and Elk Rivers. This recreational area is where they saw canoeing, kayaking, whitewater rafting, and fishing.

"What kind of fish are in this river?" asked Tyler.

Rainbow trout, brown trout, and smallmouth bass mostly," responded Matthew. "Now I'll take you to the Gorge where the river drops as it enters Tennessee. It's one of the most beautiful stretches in the basin. Parts of the basin are crisscrossed by the scenic Blue Ridge Parkway and are in the Pisgah National Forest." The sailboat tour of the river lasted the entire afternoon.

As the sun was setting, Matthew said, "Sorry, everyone, but I must get back. I have some work to do before tomorrow."

Everyone got off the boat at the dock in front of the cabin and thanked Matthew for the tour.

Homer walked his cousin to his car and said, "Thanks for the tour, Matthew. I gotta question. Do ye remember if the sheriff or his deputy did a decent sweep of Stephanie's office? There was nothing in the file notes he gave me about their collecting evidence from her office. The only thing I found was a description of the room in shambles and a photograph. There was nothing about DNA collection. I was just wondering."

Homer, to be honest, I've been living in a fog since her disappearance, and I don't know the answer to your question."

"That's okay, Matthew. We'll take it from here and update ye every week."

"Wow, Homer! That's wonderful! The sheriff never updated us on the case unless we asked him for details. Thank you!!" He was so overcome with gratitude that he hugged Homer.

As Homer entered the cabin, he saw Victoria in the kitchen, and whatever it was she was cooking grabbed his nose! "Somethang smells real good, Victoria," he said as he walked over to where she was standing.

"Victoria, you, and Zach weren't asked here so that the cooking would be your job. Ye know that I done got a little bit of money squirreled away," he said, grinning. "We can go to McDonald's or to a nice eatin' place, or have supper delivered here, or whatever ye want. Zach needs to help us with the legal stuff, and he's a whiz on the computer keepin' up with what we do, but ye, young lady, are here to sit back, read, walk along the water, or shop. Ye got what I'm tryin' to say, Victoria?"

"I do, but you need to know that Zach and I love you, Homer, and we want to do things for you." Victoria surprised Homer when she gave him a big hug.

Tears welled up, and Homer replied, "Well then. Let's chow down!"

During supper, Brayden said, "Homer, I know you are glad to have your dog back with you. Did they tell you what Duke learned while in police training?"

"Yep. Duke learned some pretty cool thangs fer a dog. One of the thangs will be put to the test real soon. He learnt how to find a dead body. It don't matter if the body is in a grave or on the bottom of the river.

"Six weeks is way too long for this case to still be open. She might be alive, but I doubt it. If she's dead, her body might not be in Watauga County, but on the other hand, it might be. We need to git goin' on this case, so I think it's time to let our newest team member help us. I was told that Duke was a quick learner and did real good in his training."

Tom and Homer were deep in conversation the following day when Zach interrupted and asked if he could drive them to the church to start evidence collecting in Stephanie's office.

THE LOGBOOK

"You're the right guy to go with us, Zach. As our lawyer, I want ye to write up everthang we know so far. It would hep if ye typed up Stephanie went missin' six weeks ago, and we took the investigation away from the Watauga County Sheriff's Department who started the investigation and not us. Your notes gotta tell the whole story 'bout what ye see and any evidence we git. Zach don't be tempted to guess 'bout what coulda happened unless ye are real sure what did happen. Bring the camera with ye and take shots of her office and anything we think could be helpful," said Homer.

"You should tell Victoria that we might be late tonight, or at the least, we might miss supper, so she should save us something to eat.

"We'll go over every square inch of Stephanie's office to find even the smallest clue. Zach, label and identify all evidence we hand you. Be sure that physical evidence is collected, put in evidence bags, labeled, and dated – let's make sure we don't leave anything behind. The three of us will make a final walk-through to be sure that all potential evidence is bagged and tagged," Tom instructed Zach.

"Thanks for including me, guys. The investigation will be a great learning experience for me, and I appreciate how you're allowing me to help," Zach said.

"Zach, it's not a matter of 'allowing ye to help.' Ye are a big part of the team, and we need a lawyer like ye. "Okay, let's git this thang goin'. Zach, here's the stuff that the sheriff gave us yesterday. Let's take it with us,'" instructed Homer. "Ready, Tom?"

THE LOGBOOK

"You bet, Homer."

"I don't think I need to take Duke with us 'til we're happy with what we see and git from Stephanie's office. It maybe tomorrow before he gits to come with us. Okay, everybody, we'll stay in touch. Please don't call us unless it is important. Thanks.

"Zach, git whatever ye need to take with ye 'cause we don't want to have to stop and come back to git somethang," Homer said.

Zach took about ten minutes to gather what he needed, then came downstairs lugging his laptop in its case.

"Do you want to drive, Zach?" asked Tom.

"Sure," he replied.

Homer said, "Great, then let's get this show on the road!"

Zach kissed his wife goodbye, and then the three men went to the church.

Pastor Henry was in his office and heard the men coming in the back door. He met them in the hallway and said, "I plan to be here until at least noon. If you need anything, just let me know. I won't interrupt you while you're working because I know this is important, and I certainly don't want to hinder you."

"Thanks, Pastor White, we appreciate your cooperation," said Tom.

"Pastor White, what is the name of your new secretary?" asked Homer.

I guess his name is Pastor White," he said with a laugh. "The Finance Committee determined that since the tithes and offerings are low, we cannot afford to hire a secretary. I have yet to find a church volunteer to help in this area.

That's ok I understand that women are busy, we have no secretary at present."

"Thanks, pastor. We just didn't want to interrupt someone's workday," Homer responded.

As the men strolled down the hallway towards Stephanie's office, Zach commented, "I feel like we're in a movie. Like *Men in Black*." Everyone laughed, which helped relieve the tension.

About two hours into their investigation, Homer thumbed through a few books on a shelf beside Stephanie's desk. He reached for one, and when he opened it, he realized it was her daily logbook where she kept personal notes in addition to her daily schedule. Thinking he may have hit on something potentially important, he sat down and started reading the most recent entries.

He learned that it was part of Stephanie's job every Monday morning to unlock the alms and offering boxes located on the wall at the back of the auditorium. She would remove the cash and checks and record the contributions made by church members. Homer noticed that about two months ago, she wrote in her book that she had observed there was never cash in the boxes.

She wrote, *Someone must be stealing from the church. I checked the boxes, and it doesn't look like*

THE LOGBOOK

someone has pried them open, so does that mean that someone has a key?

Homer made a note of this entry.

Not every page in her logbook contained potentially usable information regarding Stephanie's disappearance. There were prayer requests she recorded from church members, but nothing red-flagged by Homer.

A person called Stephanie asking for the church to pray for her elderly, sick mother who had a stomach virus.

Another entry was regarding prayer for a woman's husband who had been collecting tree limbs and other debris off their property. Unfortunately, a stick hit him in the eye, and his wife had to take him to the Eye Foundation Hospital.

The entry on the next page really caught Homer's attention. It was from Sharon Smith, who was asking for prayer for her husband, Rex.

The entry read, "Sharon Smith called today requesting prayer for her husband. Sharon said that when her husband came home from work and read the mail, he discovered her spending habits were off the chart. He took her credit cards and checkbook away to stop her from spending. Sharon was ashamed of her habit and requested prayer to reunite her and her husband. Rex told her that he would do whatever it took to climb out of this debt."

Homer believed that her logbook would be vital to finding out what happened to Stephanie. After reading one of her entries, it seemed to Homer that for some reason, Stephanie was reluctant to report that someone was stealing money from the church. Homer could only assume she didn't want to blame a fellow church member or someone else she knew, so she held this information tightly to her chest.

Since Pastor White told him earlier that the church couldn't afford to hire another secretary, he wondered if the pastor was aware someone had been stealing. Homer made a note to discuss this with Pastor White.

Chapter 4
Duke, track!

Homer stopped reading and said, "Tom, I think I've just stumbled on somethang that could have some whoppin' clues fer us." He held the book up and said, "This here is Stephanie's daily logbook; it's got prayer requests from church members. This logbook has lots ah notes, and she done wrote down all 'bout what happened to people. I think it's sad, but it seems ever durn story I read people were desperate for money. We need to talk to these folks 'cause Stephanie thought somebody was stealing money from the offering and alms boxes. Our person of interest could be someone on this list. I'm goin' to finish reading what Stephanie wrote and then give you the book."

"Great, then we'll compare notes and decide what direction to take."

Homer had to skip several pages she wrote about church members with requests ranging from dogs running away to people losing jobs. Finally, he came across a request she had recorded that seemed important.

"Stephanie's notes just opened a can of worms. Now, my cousin Matthew joins the list of possible people of interest." Homer began reading the entry.

I need to pray for Matthew. I don't know what he was thinking. We've been saving for a year to go to Scotland and Ireland for our anniversary. Matthew spent our trip money to buy his new truck! He promised he'd do anything and everything to get the money in time for us to go.

I needed to talk to someone about what Matthew did, so I called Mary Beth. Instead of telling her how disappointed and broken hearted I was about Matthew, she

DUKE, TRACK!

Started telling me her problems. I knew I needed to listen and decided to talk to her later.

Mary Beth told me not to tell anyone about her husband's gambling, but I did want to write it down so I could pray for their marriage and especially that her husband would stop gambling. Her husband, Leon, had gambled them into $34,000 in debt.

When Homer turned the page, he realized the entry on this page was the last one Stephanie made in her logbook.

Homer's train of thought vanished when Tom asked, "Any leads, Homer?"

"Lots of 'em! Let's git some coffee, and I'll fill ye in," said Homer with a grin.

"I honestly don't know how you do it, Homer. You are a born detective! Right off the bat, the first place we look, you have a possible reason for what may have happened to Mrs. Wright, and people that need to be interviewed!" commented Zach.

"So, what now?" asked Tom.

"I reckon we start talkin' to some people," answered Homer. "Do you have any nerve-racking skills you want to teach me to git somebody to fess up, Tom?"

"Maybe, but why don't we take that logbook with us and study it some more in detail back at the cabin?" suggested Tom.

"There ye go, Tom!" Homer replied.

"Not so fast, guys. We should plan to come back here tomorrow. I need to take some pictures first, including that book in your hand, Homer, and it needs to be documented as evidence. When I'm finished in a few minutes, we can go back to the cabin," commented Zach.

"It's great that we have a lawyer on the team!" said Tom. "He keeps us straight!"

"Tom, while Zach is doing his job, I'd like for ye to see if ye can git some fingerprints from the offering and alms boxes," instructed Homer. "Let's see who can open them boxes since Stephanie's disappeared.

"I think I done heard the pastor leave a while ago. I'm going to call him. I need to tell him about the people we're going to hire. A few minutes ago, I called a Forensic Accounting outfit that's gonna meet us here tomorrow, and I want to chat with Pastor White about it," commented Homer.

"What kind of an accounting firm is that?" asked Zach.

"I'm gonna hire Forensic Accounting Services in Asheville. Gary Cleveland's gonna be working with us to see just how much money got stole," answered Homer.

"To answer your question, a forensic accounting firm uses accounting, auditing, and investigative skills to examine the finances of a business," added Tom.

"This case is fascinating, and I'm learning a lot!" Zach said.

Forty-five minutes later, Zach gathered his computer and several notebooks and pens he brought for everyone. He placed Stephanie's logbook in one of the evidence bags he brought in case they were needed. While Homer locked the church, Zach loaded everything in the car, then slipped Behind the steering wheel. Homer and Tom laughed when they got to the car and saw Zach was packed and ready to go back to the cabin.

It was 6:45 p.m. when they arrived at the cabin. The team had waited to have supper together to hear about Homer, Tom, and Zach's day. During supper, they were given an update.

"Tomorrow, everyone except Victoria's gits to go with us to the church. Duke even gets to come along. We'll leave here early, somewhere around seven. Guys, be ready on time," Homer insisted.

"Victoria, this is your chance to go shopping! Here is Matthew's phone number. He'll have a lady from the church fetch you and show you around town. Have fun.

"Goodnight, folks. Duke, let's take a walk." A few minutes later, Homer and Duke came back inside and disappeared down the hall to Homer's room.

Tyler said, "I can't wait to see Duke in action tomorrow! Wouldn't it be great if he finds Stephanie? I don't think she ran out on Matthew, and I'm sorry to say that I believe someone took her life."

"That's what I've been thinking, too," Brayden said. "Well, I'm going to call it a night. I want to be rested for tomorrow. Good night, guys, and Mrs. Thomas."

After Brayden left the room, everyone else decided to call it a night, too. Soon, all lights in the cabin were out, except the lamp in the living room.

DUKE, TRACK!

The following day, everyone assembled in the living room and waited for Homer to end his conversation with Tom

And give them his instructions. Realizing the room got quiet, Homer ended his chat and joined the others.

"Zach, I want you and Tyler to meet Gary Cleveland with the forensic accounting folks. Then make sure he meets Pastor White. Tell the pastor what these guys will be doing. Also, tell the pastor that Mr. Cleveland plans to take the church's financial books with him to Asheville. If there is a problem, find Tom or me. Brayden, I want you to be in Stephanie's office with Tom and me, helping us find clues and stuff. Y'all got any questions?

"Okay, seeing there's not any, let's skedaddle," Homer said as he put Duke in the back area of their rented Chevy Suburban.

Tyler asked Zach, "Could you hear what Homer and Tom were talking about back there?"

"No, I wasn't standing close enough. Why?"

"I just thought they were secretive. It may just be my imagination."

They arrived at the church and Homer unlocked the back door. He and Tom stayed back to let Duke walk before going inside.

Tom opened their conversation by asking, "So after Stephanie's last entry in her logbook, there was a page torn out? Do you think it could have been coincidental or on purpose?"

"You were the one who told me if I'm not sure, don't guess. I think it's weird, don't you? I wanted you to know so we can be aware of our surroundings and not take

DUKE, TRACK!

anything for granted," replied Homer. "For now, let's keep this to ourselves."

"There is technology to see if there was an indentation on the following page that may show what was written," said Tom.

"Let's wait on that to see if we're gonna need it," replied Homer.

It was a busy morning with the accounting firm coming and collecting information, the pastor asking questions, several people in Stephanie's office looking for evidence. The team had asked several city policemen to come today and walk around the church looking for clues. Duke was also looking for clues. Homer had taken the leash off his dog's collar and allowed him to roam in anticipation he would find evidence of Stephanie's blood, or anything else pertinent to the case.

After Duke had sniffed for evidence in Stephanie's office and the hallway, he came back into the office where Homer was sitting. Duke sat in front of him and laid his head in Homer's lap. He looked at him with sad eyes. Homer stroked his dog and said, "Good boy, Duke."

Homer turned to Tom and commented, "Duke didn't find nothin', and I think he's disappointed. I wish I could tell him that it's been six-weeks and smells he would detect are likely gone. Homer looked at Duke again and handed him a treat he had in his pocket. "Good dog, Duke." His dog took the treat and sat in the corner with his reward.

Suddenly, Duke sprung to his feet and barked once. He had laid down next to Stephanie's open purse. He was sniffing her hairbrush when Homer realized what he was doing.

Tom, why don't we take Stephanie's hairbrush with us? It is possible we can use the hairbrush whenever we search for Stephanie."

"Great idea, Homer. Do it!" replied Tom.

"Don't forget, we have to document that we are taking it," Zach reminded them.

Homer's phone rang. It was Matthew.

"Homer, I know you are busy, but I thought I'd make a suggestion. Take a break for lunch. Grab some Chick-Fil-A sandwiches and drinks and drive out the old dirt road near the church. It is about a quarter of a mile on the same side as the church. It is a rugged and narrow road, but passable.

About a half-mile down the road, it dead ends at Wilbur Lake.

"Three miles below Watauga Dam, on the Horseshoe section of the Watauga River, is the TVA Wilbur Dam, forming a much smaller but extremely deep reservoir known as Wilbur Lake. There are a few picnic tables there and I think it would be a wonderful place to take your team to clear their heads while eating lunch. I think everyone would enjoy the scenery. I hope you'll consider going there."

"Thanks. I think we'll take you up on that thar suggestion. Can you come with us?" asked Homer.

"Sorry, I have a pile of work on my desk to finish and a meeting with the teachers after school. Before becoming a principal, I taught high school history. I had no idea how hard a principal's job was. It's not very glamorous, either."

"Baloney! I'm proud of you, cousin, for working with teachers and kids. I'm sure Stephanie was proud of you, too. Gotta go, Matthew. We're busier than a blind dog in a meat house," Homer said and ended their call.

After several hours working, Zach asked, "Homer, when do we eat? I'm starved."

"Okay, I'm 'bout as hungry as all git out, too. Let's round up the team and grab some grub at Chick-Fil-A. I'll meet you in the car. Me and Duke need to take a stroll."

After everyone was in the car, Homer told them about having a picnic at Wilbur Lake. "I'm glad we're here in North Carolina. It's plum purty, ain't it?"

They all agreed. Everyone got a Chick-Fil-A sandwich and headed down the road.

Duke was enjoying the ride in the back of the car. Brayden once had a dog that loved to hang his head out the window, so he decided to see what Duke would do. Brayden rolled down the window and Duke immediately hung his head out and let the breeze blow his face. Duke loved it.

They had only driven a short distance when Duke started barking and pacing in the back of the Suburban. Brayden laughed and said that Duke smelled the sandwiches and wanted the first bite. Everyone laughed. Brayden calmed Duke and they continued down the road.

Once at Wilbur Lake, Brayden found an ideal picnic table beside the water. He grabbed the chicken sandwiches and handed them out along with the drinks.

DUKE, TRACK!

While everyone was enjoying the scenery or helping set the table, Homer pulled Brayden aside.

"Brayden, I've been watching you on this trip, and I've seen a more grown-up team member. Thanks for all the help you're giving me. Attention to detail is what makes a good detective. Passing the test and gitting a license is one thang but having a sense of being part of a team is a lot more valuable. Thanks," Homer said and extended his hand.

"I wasn't aware that I was doing that, but it sure feels good to have you say that I'm doing things the way you like," said Brayden flashing a big smile.

Once everyone was seated, Homer said, "Today, Duke is supposed to show us what he learned."

"Please tell us more about that, Homer," said Zach.

"Auburn University done told me that a graduate of K-9 police training is a super-officer. Duke can jump higher than most men and run twice as fast. His eyes are good enough to see in the dark, he can hear 'bout anythang, he can bark loud enough to wake the dead. But Duke's true glory is his nose. He can smell a dead body fifteen feet in a grave and thirty feet underwater. Duke can and will find Stephanie," Homer said proudly.

When they finished lunch, they headed back to the church. As Zach approached the area where Duke barked and jumped on the way to Wilbur Lake, Duke started the same behavior.

"Homer, let's put a lease on Duke and let him walk around in this area. What do you think?" asked Tom.

"Great idea."

DUKE, TRACK!

Zach stopped, and Tom and Homer got out of the car. Duke jumped from the car when Homer called him. He was told to heel so Homer could put a leash on his harness. Duke had smelled Stephanie's hairbrush while at the church. Homer brought it with him and let Duke smell it again.

"Track," said Homer. He was practically pulled to the ground by his excited dog. "I guess Duke's training has kicked in!" Homer said. He told Duke, "Track" as he dropped the leash.

Within a few minutes, Duke stopped, wagged his tail excitedly, and then laid quietly down. Duke continued to wag his tail when Homer approached him.

"What did you find, buddy? Let's have a look.

"Good dog, good dog," Homer said as he patted Duke's head.

Homer said, "Show me." Duke started digging at the edge of the grave, then laid down. Homer reached in his pocket and gave a dog treat to Duke. "Good dog, Duke," he said again to his dog and gave him a hug.

"It sure seems to me that Duke has sniffed something important, maybe even the odor of a corpse, and look here," Homer said as he pointed to where Duke laid down. "This area even looks like a grave.

"Let's tape off the area," Homer said as he instructed the team. "Tom, would you call the Boone Police Department and the Watauga Sheriff's Office and let 'em know we done found a place in the woods that looks kinda like a grave, and, who knows? It could possibly be Stephanie's."

"Not a problem, Homer," replied Tom.

A Boone policeman arrived first and was greeted by Homer and Brayden. Within minutes a sheriff's department investigator joined the men.

"Hey, Gene," the deputy said to the officer and extended his hand.

"Hello, Steven."

"Here's the spot we called ye about. We didn't touch nothing, so you can take it from here. We'll just watch," said Homer.

"How was this area found and what made you suspect it was a grave?" asked Gene.

"My dog, Duke. He's had cadaver dog training," answered Homer. "Matthew Wright gave us his wife's hairbrush when I told him we'd be using my dog in the investigation. Today, we had the hairbrush with us, so I let Duke smell it, then told him to 'track.' He found this spot real quick."

"That's wonderful, Mr. Yancey. We hope to have a K-9 unit the first of the year. Was your dog trained at Auburn University?" asked Officer Hinkle.

"Yes. This is Duke. Duke, shake hands." Duke sat and lifted his paw to shake the officer's hand.

"Impressive, Mr. Yancey. Now, let's see what Duke found."

Both lawmen went to the suspicious site a few feet away and immediately noticed variations in the surface and depressions in the soil.

DUKE, TRACK!

Homer watched intently as the men used ground-penetrating radar to image the subsurface.

The lawmen noticed Homer's interest, so they began explaining the procedure so Homer could take notes. The men put on evidence collecting gloves and meticulously removed leaves and dirt. **Ten minutes** later, they found a body.

"What do we have here?" asked the coroner who had just arrived at the scene. In addition to being the coroner, he is also the Watauga Medical Examiner.

"A deceased female, with a bullet hole in the head. It could possibly be the remains of Stephanie Wright, who disappeared about six weeks ago," responded Gene. "She's all yours, Jerry!"

"I'll call forensics, and they'll come for the body. We will also give them the bullet found in the grave. They will hold this evidence until the gun is found and sent to them for comparative analyses. After their forensic examination, we'll be able to provide the identity of the deceased, the cause of death and any other pertinent information you may need," commented Coroner Kent. "Mr. Yancey, I read in the newspaper that your firm, Yancey Investigative Services, is investigating this case. Is that correct?"

Homer replied, "Yeah we've been hired by Matthew to investigate the disappearance and possible death of his wife."

"Mr. Yancey, since that is the case, the forensic report will be sent to you. Do you have a business card I can have?" the coroner asked.

Homer gave the coroner his card.

The coroner turned his back to the men and placed a call to forensic. About an hour later, forensics arrived with a body bag. The body was laid on a gurney and positioned in the back of a van. The coroner informed everyone that The North Carolina State Crime Laboratory in Raleigh would perform the autopsy.

It was a long day for the Yancey team, and it was sunset before they left the crime scene. When they parked in front of their cabin, Victoria ran outside to meet the team.

"I've been worried about you. Is everything okay?" Victoria asked.

"We'll tell you about it over supper. We're starved," responded Zach.

"I've been shopping all day, so I just picked up some sandwiches from Chick-Fil-A."

Everyone laughed.

Chapter 5
Gotcha, Homer

During supper, the team updated Victoria and discussed what they planned to do next with the investigation. The consensus was to continue to follow the leads provided in Stephanie's logbook and to check in with the auditing firm.

"Zach, how are things going on the legal end? Have you documented everything and properly marked all evidence?" asked Tom.

"Tom, I could use some help. There is a lot involved in properly documenting and labeling evidence. Plus, we are required to register and comply with the North Carolina Department of Public Safety. That is truly a time-consuming procedure. Do you want me to continue with my list?" asked Zach.

"Yes, by all means," responded Tom.

"Ok. There is the legal research to be done. I need to make certain that the documentation regarding the remains Duke found are accurate and submitted properly to the State. I will also be working with the North Carolina State Crime Lab. I have no idea at this point how much time that will require. In addition, I will be documenting the upcoming interviews of the individuals mentioned in Stephanie's logbook," Zach said.

"Thank you for sharing exactly what you will be responsible for and how much of your time it will require. Homer and I have noticed signs that you might be feeling overwhelmed, and we certainly don't want you to be stressed. We were pretty sure you needed another attorney to help you, so we hired one to work with you. You'll be responsible for delegating responsibilities to her," Tom commented.

"Who is she?" asked Zach.

"Amelia McGuire Davis. She's Brayden's sister. She's a hard worker and an excellent lawyer."

"When do you think Amelia can start?"

"She'll be arriving here tomorrow. You and Victoria can show her around, and you can update her on this case. If you feel uncomfortable working with a woman, you have our permission to take Victoria with you while you work. However, I want you to know that we're not hiring Victoria, so please explain that to her. Also, tell Victoria that she is not to think she can speculate or investigate with us. Without her having a license, our firm could be in a lot of trouble. Understood?" emphasized Tom.

"Yes, and I'll explain that to Victoria."

The following day at breakfast, Homer asked, "Brayden, when do we start questionin' our first person of interest?"

"We'll meet Rex and Sharon Smith at 10:00 a.m. in the pastor's office. He'll not be in the office today and said that we can do our interview there. I thought it would be best to have both present for the questioning because we're not sure which one could be stealing from the church."

Tom commented, "Since I used to teach this stuff, I'm curious how you convinced them to come in for questioning."

"I told them that we are now the lead detectives in this case. Also, since it has been over six weeks since Stephanie disappeared, we thought talking to them might help clear up some confusion. I told the couple that we'd appreciate it if both would be willing to help us out."

"Excellent, Brayden!" Tom said and patted Brayden on the back.

Homer spoke up. "I'm gonna take Tom, Zach, and Tyler to be with me today when we talk to the Smiths. Brayden why don't ye call the North Carolina State Crime Lab in Raleigh 'bout when they're gonna send us that thar forensics report.

"Okay, any questions?" **Homer asked.**

There were none.

"Okay then, I've got somethang to say. I told y'all we'd have fun and work while we're here. Since we'll have a new person comin' onboard today to help with this here investigation, I think it'd be a nice welcome fer her if we have a cookout this afternoon down by the water. Ain't it nice we got this big ole cabin right beside the Watauga

River? We can eat early, then go fer another sailboat ride. Are y'all okay with this idea?" asked Homer.

"Is that a serious question?" asked Brayden.

Everyone laughed.

"Great, then let's git movin.' We've done got work to do," Homer said.

Homer, Tom, Zach, and Tyler were in the pastor's office when the Smiths arrived. After brief introductions, Homer thanked the Smiths for their willingness to come and talk to them. Homer then handed the questioning off to Tom.

"How well did you know Stephanie Wright?" asked Tom.

"We were pretty good friends," answered Sharon, who was constantly shifting positions in her chair.

"So, tell us about your friendship," said Tyler.

"Well, she and I would go to lunch at least once a month and just have 'girl time.'"

"Mrs. Smith, I can see that you are nervous. Please relax. We know that some people who watch police stories on television think that if someone is called in for questioning that they might end up being arrested for a crime they didn't commit. First of all, we are private investigators and do not have the authority to arrest people. We merely asked you here today because it has been over six weeks since Stephanie disappeared, and we still have not solved her case. We are hoping you can help us get to know her better and use that information to find out where she is or if there is reason to believe that something bad has happened to her. So, just relax, please," Tyler said.

Sharon smiled and said, "Stephanie and I've known each other for about five years. We have confided in each other, celebrated birthdays together, and have become very close. It hurts my heart that she is missing, and I pray she's still alive somewhere," Sharon said and started crying.

"Mr. Smith, would you mind stepping outside for a few minutes with Tyler and allow us to talk to you and your wife one at a time?" Tyler stood and opened the door to wait on Mr. Smith to stand. They left the room together. They went to the sanctuary and waited until Mr. Smith was called.

"Now, Sharon, what were some of the secrets you told Stephanie about?" asked Homer.

"Nothing really," she said defensively.

Tom stood and paced a few times. "Mrs. Smith, we're aware that your spending habits got out of hand at one point. Could you tell us about that, please?"

"How did you know about that?" she said with a surprised expression.

Tom ignored her question.

"Would you please tell us about it?" Tom repeated.

"But it sounds like I'm ratting on my husband if I tell you about it. I can't do that!"

"Mrs. Smith, if you choose not to answer our questions, then the suspicion becomes stronger against you and your husband. Unfortunately, we'll be forced to have the sheriff's office request from the Watauga County

Magistrate Cindy Massey to issue arrest warrants for both of you. Then we'll conduct an interrogation in which you'll have little choice but to answer our questions. Do you understand?" asked Tom. "Now, what is it going to be? Will you answer our questions now or later?"

"I get the point, Mr. Lynch. I'll answer your question. Rex came home from work one evening and when he walked in the kitchen door, he reached for the day's mail on the counter. That's when I walked into the room, and he nearly bit my head off! He asked if I was wearing another new outfit, to which I replied, 'Yes.' Then he wanted to know if we had a new refrigerator, and again, I answered, 'Yes." He was more upset at me than I had ever seen him. He stormed off, walking down our hallway, then came back and demanded that I get my purse. I refused. He became mad, so I went to our bedroom, and after finding my purse, I brought it back into the kitchen. When I attempted to hand it to him, he looked at me and insisted that I pour my purse's contents onto the counter. I did, and that's when he took all my credit cards and my checkbook. He held up all the bills that were in the mail."

Sharon continued and told us that her husband stepped closer to her and said, "Sharon, if you don't get your spending under control, we'll be in the poor house! We don't have enough money to pay our bills this month."

Then he hugged me and said, "I'm doing this because I love you. Be assured, I'll do whatever it takes to get us out of debt."

"That's all I remember, Mr. Lynch," Sharon cried.

"Thank you, Mrs. Smith. Zach, did you get all that?" commented Tom.

"All of it, Tom."

Homer said, "Zach, go get Mr. Smith and stay with him so you can record his comments. I will take Mrs. Smith to the kitchen and stay with her while we have a cup of coffee. Are you ok with that?

"Sounds good, Homer," Zach replied.

The questioning of Mr. Smith went well. He confirmed the story his wife told of their argument.

"Do you have any questions, Mr. Smith?" Tom asked.

"No. I do hope you find Stephanie," Rex replied.

After the examination, Mr. Smith was told his wife was in the church kitchen and that their cooperation was appreciated. Mr. Smith was also informed that he and his wife were free to go, but the team reserved the right to recall them should further questioning be warranted.

When Tom, Tyler, Zach, and Homer were alone in the pastor's office, Homer spoke up. "Guys, you were great. It looks to me like we have several people of interest in this case."

"We can thank Stephanie for the logbook. I think it is going to prove to be invaluable in this case," Tom said.

"Tom's right. Zach do you have all your stuff together?" Homer asked.

Zach had his hands full and gave Homer a nod.

"I know it goes without saying, but all of you know that Brayden's sister, Amelia, arrived today. She is now officially a team member, so let's show her what a great team this is," Homer said with a grin.

"Let's go have some fun!" Zach said.

Meanwhile in another location, an unidentified man laughed as he said, "Expect the unexpected, and whenever possible, be the unexpected."

He drove onto a dirt road posted with a sign clearly marked, "Private Property", and parked his car in the grass. He checked his surroundings and put on shoe coverings and gloves before getting out of the vehicle. He then stepped into the woods, walking slowly and deliberately to ensure he was undetected.

He discovered the perfect spot to carry out his mission. He was in undergrowth across the river from the Yancey team enjoying a cookout in front of their cabin. He waited until dusk so the lighting would be to his advantage when he left the woods.

GOTCHA, HOMER

He loaded his .223 rifle with his gloved hand, took aim, and waited for Homer to be in his scope. "Gotcha, Homer. Mr. Yancey, this should slow your nosey investigation down," he said as he moved his finger off the trigger guard and onto the trigger.

With Homer in sight, he pulled the trigger. Just as the rifle fired, Homer moved and the bullet hit Victoria, who was standing behind him. She screamed, fell to the ground, groaning and bleeding profusely from her upper right side. Everyone dropped to the ground because they did not know if the shot was intentional or a stray hunter's bullet.

Zach bravely sat beside his wife. "Honey, I'm calling 911. Be strong and don't leave me! Help will be here soon, and we'll go to the hospital together."

Homer grabbed Zach's phone just as 911 answered.

"Hello? I'm Homer Yancey, and a woman in our group was just shot. One of our guys just checked her out and done told me she's bleeding real bad and is going into shock. She's really messed up and we gotta get her to the hospital quick. We're at the Daniel Boone Park in Cabin 17. Please send help quick!"

The river was close, so Tyler crawled to its edge to see if anyone was there. The encroaching darkness prevented him from seeing anyone.

To Zach, it seemed like an eternity, but because the town of Boone was near the park, help arrived in less than ten minutes.

Homer commented, "The Town of Boone is on the ball! I can hear the ambulance and fire truck coming. Do you hear 'em sirens, Victoria? They're coming to help you. Hang in there."

GOTCHA, HOMER

The paramedics, a firetruck, an ambulance, a Boone police car, and a Watauga Sheriff's Department vehicle came into view, so everyone got out of the way. The first one on the scene was a Boone policeman, so Zach flagged him down and led him to Victoria lying on the ground in a pool of blood. When the policeman saw her, he radioed the ambulance driver and told him where the injured was lying and instructed him to be prepared to transport her to the hospital stat!

Immediately behind the sheriff department's car were the paramedics and the ambulance. Zach was told he would have to meet them at the hospital. After a quick exam and applying pressure to Victoria's wound, they started an IV in each arm before loading her onto a gurney and placing her in the back of the ambulance.

Tyler yelled at Zach and said, "Come on, get in."

Tyler and Zach followed the ambulance to the Watauga Medical Center Emergency Room. A nurse saw Tyler and Zach as they hurried into the ER through the ambulance entrance. She stopped them as they were trying to follow the ambulance EMTs into the trauma bay.

"Wait here, please," she said, then turned to talk to the two EMTs who needed to provide information about Victoria. The nurse introduced herself to Tyler and Zach. Her name was Regina Smith, and she immediately put them at ease. Like most Emergency Rooms, it was busy. For this reason, Regina instructed Zach and Tyler to wait in an area out of the way of the busy emergency room staff. She took insurance and other information from Zach about his wife and told him that the doctor would come and talk to him as soon as he finished examining Victoria.

Within minutes, Dr. Wilson found Zach and informed him that in a few minutes Victoria would be going to the second floor to the surgical suite to repair the damage caused by the bullet. The doctor allowed Zach to briefly visit Victoria in the exam room.

Nurse Regina came in and said, "Mr. Thomas, you, and your friend will need to go to the SICU waiting room on the fourth floor. The surgeon, Dr. John Smith, will come out and talk to you as soon as your wife is in recovery. I know you are nervous, and perhaps scared, Mr. Thomas, but be assured, your wife is in good hands."

Even though Victoria was in a lot of pain, she squeezed Zach's hand. He gave her a kiss just before she was hastily wheeled away. Zach walked out of the exam room and saw the entire Yancey team standing with Tyler by the exit door. He walked over to them and hugged Homer.

Trying to remain brave, Zach said, "We have to wait on the fourth floor in the SICU waiting room."

"Zach, before we go, let's pray for Victoria," said Homer. Chaplain Joe Hollis overheard Homer and asked to pray with them. He asked God for grace, strength, and mercy.

After praying, the chaplain could see that the men deeply cared for Zach and Victoria. He said, "If we pray a prayer in faith, then we must believe the Lord heard our prayer and will answer." The Chaplain turned to Zach and said, "As long as we have God, we have hope." Everyone nodded in agreement.

GOTCHA, HOMER

After an hour in the SICU waiting room, Homer whispered to Tom, "Don't ye think we ought to do some detective work and see if the shooter got sloppy and left some clues? We gotta find out who done this and why. Who were they really tryin' to shoot and why? I done got some doubts they was trying to hurt Victoria! I know we need to be here fer Zach, but we need to find and git us the person who tried to kill Victoria. It would be very hard to leave Zach right now. Whatcha think, Tom?"

"Let's just ask him, Homer."

"Zach, Homer, and I want to go back and do some investigating to see if we can learn anything regarding who shot Victoria. We need to return to the crime scene while the trail is still hot, so to speak. If you had rather, we can stay here with you and do our investigating later," Tom explained.

"Please go! There's not a lot you can do here while we sit around and wait. Tom, this is the best investigative team on planet earth, and I need you to find out who did this to my wife. She could be fighting for her life because of some dirtbag," Zach said.

"Zach, somebody needs to call us as soon as the doctor tells you how she's a doin'. I mean it, okay?" Homer said with a serious expression.

"You guys check in with us, too," Brayden said, then added, "Please find the dirtbag!"

Tom and Homer left the hospital and took the first turn leading to the bridge across the Watauga River. Homer used the map to locate the cluster of cabins along the river in the area where they were staying. Homer studied the map while Tom drove. Homer found on the map the restricted road that was on the opposite side of the river from the cabins. The gate to the road was open, so they drove in.

The woods and underbrush were thick, and even using their bright flashlight, they could not see which cabin was theirs until Homer shouted, "Stop! That cabin looks like thar's been a cookout in the front yard. Looks like they been cookin' on them BBQ grills, and thar are plates and food rite thar on the tables, but thar ain't nobody outside. That's gotta be our place."

Tom stopped the car and parked in the grass. He opened the door to get out, but Homer pulled his arm back. "We've got to look down for any clues, tire prints, footprints, broke twigs, anything, but specially casings," Homer said.

"I wasn't thinking. 'The student has become the Master,'" Tom said, bringing a smile to Homer's face.

Both men had flashlights and used them to look for casings or other clues as they walked slowly and carefully to the river's edge. They were unable to find a single clue.

Chapter Six
Forensic Report

"Tom, don't you think we oughta call the law and ask if they found anything? They might of stayed here after we took off fer the hospital." Homer said.

Tom already had the sheriff's department on the phone. He told them he was with Yancey Investigative Services and asked for information regarding the shooting at Cabin 17. He was transferred to Steven Adamson's extension.

He answered, "Detective Adamson."

"Detective, this is Tom Lynch with Yancey Investigative Services. Do you have a minute?"

"Good to hear from you, Mr. Lynch. How is Mrs. Thomas? Is she going to be all right?" asked the detective.

"She was still in surgery when we left the hospital. She's in serious condition right now. Thanks for asking about her. The purpose of my call is to see if you or anyone else was able to go across the river to look for evidence possibly left by the person who shot Victoria?" Tom asked. "Homer Yancey and I are in the area now where we believe the shooter took aim and shot Victoria. It looks like a clean sweep here."

"You're right. We found nothing unusual and no shell casings. I have a man staking out that area and he notified me when you drove up. I guess you'd have already been placed in one of our cells here except that he recognized you, Mr. Lynch, when you got out of the vehicle. I wanted him to stay there, hidden, in case someone returned to the scene. Just to make certain there is not another incident, we will have four of our deputies guarding your cabin tonight," the detective told the men.

FORENSIC REPORT

"Mr. Lynch, you need to be with your team at the hospital. We have this covered and will call you immediately if anyone returns to the crime scene or if we find anything to share with you. Right now, go back to the hospital. You can trust us to handle it tonight." Detective Adamson's words were like music to their ears.

"Thanks, Detective."

Tom and Homer drove back to the hospital. When they got off the elevator on the fourth floor, they saw a Boone police officer stationed outside the SICU waiting room.

"Go on in, Mr. Yancey, Mr. Lynch," he said as they approached. "My orders come from Lieutenant Charles Douglas, a detective with the Boone Police Department. My name is Officer Bill McBrayer. If you need anything, just let me know. Your team will have protection while Mrs. Thomas is here."

Homer and Tom shook the officer's hand, who stepped aside so that they could enter the room.

"Hey guys, what did you learn? Any evidence left behind?" asked Tyler.

"First, Zach, how's **my adopted niece** doin'?" asked Homer as he sat beside him.

"She's still in surgery, Homer," he replied. "Homer, is she going to make it?"

"Zach, ye gotta be strong and hold on to hope like the chaplain said. I believe Victoria will pull through this because she has ye," Homer said with a grin.

"This is tough, but you are tougher. Take everything one day at a time. On the harder days, give me a call because I can listen when you need to talk. Zach, you are some brave dude and I know Victoria will be able to see that too. I'm proud of you," Homer said, then hugged Zach.

Just at that moment, the surgeon, Dr. Smith, walked into the waiting room. "Mr. Thomas?"

Zach stood.

"Come with me, please."

Zach asked Homer to come with him. The three men walked out into the hallway. Dr. Smith put his hand on Zach's shoulder and said, "She'll be in SICU for a few days, and we'll allow you to sit with her some during the day. When the nurses get her settled in, I'll let you see her briefly. She came through the surgery just fine. The bullet entered her right lung, then exited her body, but her injuries were severe. She was one fortunate young lady. The real issue right now is her loss of blood. She lost a lot when she was shot and also during surgery. She's in SICU because I want to observe her kidney and brain functions to make sure both remain in a normal range. I don't expect any complications, but we must be careful and monitor her around the clock. After SICU, she'll be in a room for a while until we are comfortable with her recovery. So, Mr. Thomas, in summary, keep praying for your wife.

"Give me a few minutes, Mr. Thomas, and I'll see if the nurses are ready for you to see your wife." Dr. Smith left and entered the unit, but quickly reappeared and motioned for Zach to follow him.

Zach looked at Homer, who said, "Zach, I'll wait right here fer ye. Kiss her fer me," he said with a grin.

FORENSIC REPORT

The team waited in the SICU waiting room until Zach and Homer came in to update them.

"I had an excellent conversation with Victoria's surgeon, Dr. John Smith. I asked him to please tell me everything that happened once she was brought to the Emergency Room. He was kind enough to enlighten me.

"Victoria was stabilized in what they call the trauma bay, and then she went to the operating room. I'm truly grateful to Dr. Smith and his surgical nurse, Christina, as well as the technicians that fought to save her life. Of course, I also appreciate the anesthesiologist who helped Dr. Smith.

"After Victoria's surgery, she was moved here to the SICU. I like Dr. Smith's personal attention to

Victoria and his courtesy to me. He introduced me to Dr. Mark Fowler, the SICU doctor that will manage her care here on fourth floor. He told me that Victoria would be sedated most of the time, but occasionally he will order her sedation to briefly stop so that he can determine how she does mentally. The rest was just mumbo jumbo, but I heard that we're blessed that her injuries weren't worse. The good news is Dr. Smith said that it may take time, but she will recover."

Just as Zach finished his report, his parents and Victoria's parents walked into the room. After Zach hugged them, he introduced the team.

"Nice to meet y'all, but we're gonna leave ye with Zach. We need to git some rest so we can do some investigatin' tomorrow. Good night, y'all." Homer said as he ushered the team out the door.

"Zach, I'll bring you some clothes and stuff in the morning," said Tyler.

When the elevator door opened for them, Sheriff Reed stepped off. "Homer!" the sheriff extended his hand. "Hello everyone, I wanted to come by and get an update on Mrs. Thomas. Is she going to be all right? How is Zach?"

After he received a brief update regarding Victoria's condition, he told the team that after people in the community of Watauga County heard on the news about Victoria being shot, his office was flooded with calls. People have been volunteering financial donations to be used by Zach for food or whatever he needs.

Sheriff Reed said that a bank account in Zach's name will be set up tomorrow for him.

Homer was speechless and had to turn away for a minute. "Sheriff, Zach is in the waitin' room with his parents and in-laws. I think it would be good if ye told Zach yourself about the donations. I'm sure he'll be as grateful as we are. We gotta go, but I'm sure we'll see you later," the team shook hands with the sheriff, then stepped into the elevator.

Just at that moment, Detective Adamson called to say that his men did a thorough sweep of the location where the Yancey team members were staying. He reported that they found the bullet that exited Mrs. Thomas. It was found lodged in the post holding up the deck at Homer's cabin.

FORENSIC REPORT

"Since you're the lead investigative team on this case, I'll share the evidence with you in the morning," Steven said as he ended the call.

Once back at the cabin, Homer called a meeting of the team. Homer, Tom, Tyler, Brayden, and Amelia sat in the living room and waited for Homer's instructions.

"Tomorrow, we've got a lot of work to do. We are a good investigative team, so let's figure out who shot Victoria. We also need to find Stephanie! Right now, I feel about as useful as a steering wheel on a mule," Homer said.

Tom put his hand on Homer's shoulder and said, "We'll nail both of them. We're the Yancey Investigative team and we haven't lost a case yet!"

Homer smiled.

"Brayden, Tyler, call the forensic lab so we'll know what they found out, and don't forget that there could be a thief at the church. Be sure and check that out. Brayden, I need ye to call the forensic auditors and tell 'em we want an update. So, these here are your assignments. Tell these guys we want a written report of what they found. Brayden don't you forget to include your sister in this assignment and bring her up to speed on what's going on."

"Who should we interview next, Homer?" asked Tom.

"I really don't like this, but we're gonna have to talk to Matthew. I can ask him to come down to the church tomorrow, but I don't have to tell him we are gonna ask him some hard questions," Homer said.

FORENSIC REPORT

"Guys, if I remember right, I read in Stephanie's logbook that she and Matthew had a big fight a few weeks before she disappeared. They were saving up fer a trip overseas, and Matthew confessed that he blew the money to buy a new pickup. I don't want to believe that my cousin killed his wife, but my feelings about my relative can't git in the way of this investigation," said Homer. "Tom, maybe you oughta git him to come to the church in the mornin' so we can git his side of the story."

"You bet," Tom responded.

Homer put the leash on ole Duke, and when he stepped onto the porch, he saw the two sheriff deputies he was told would be protecting them tonight.

"Hello, men," Homer said as he extended his hand.

"Mr. Yancey, we are here to protect all of you tonight. There are two more deputies in the yard with night vision binoculars to ensure no one attempts to harm you or anyone on your team. Mr. Yancey, I'm Deputy Bob Monroe, and this is my partner Deputy Matthew Smith. It's an honor to guard you tonight. On a personal note, sir, I've heard a lot about your investigative skills and they are impressive."

"Thank ye, young man. I'll leave the cabin unlocked so ye can come and git some coffee. Thank ye fer guardin' us. Come on, Duke. Time fer a walk," Homer said as he led Duke down the stairs to the front yard.

The following day, Homer updated everyone on Victoria's condition. "I called our buddy, Zach, before I went to bed last night. Dr. Smith said that since Victoria

FORENSIC REPORT

was doin' so much better, he planned to cut back on her meds. Zach said it wasn't long before she started comin' 'round. They was both happy to see each other. Of course, Victoria started asking questions, so Zach told her the whole story.

"After Victoria fell asleep, Zach said the doctor came back in and told him that due to Victoria's quick recovery, he planned to move her to a room this morning. He told me she will still have protection outside her hospital room door for a few days since we don't know if that dadgum bullet was meant fer Victoria or me." With a smirk on his face, Homer continued, "I really don't think Victoria was supposed to git shot. But I do think the shooter was trying to sidetrack us from doin' our job."

Tom said, "I totally agree, Homer."

Homer shot a smile at Tom, then said, "Okay, we've got work to do. Y'all got your assignments. Let's link up fer lunch. Let's get 'er done!"

Homer had just parked his car at the church when his phone rang.

"Homer, it's Tyler. I just got a call from forensics, and I had them text me their forensic report. Just a minute, and I'll read it to you."

> 'The victim has been positively identified as Stephanie Lynn Hicks Wright, approximately 5'2", around 120 pounds. She was rendered unconscious by a severe blow to the back of the neck. Her death resulted from a fatal wound in the left temple from a .22 caliber handgun. The full report and photos to follow.'
>
> Dr. Macy McElderry
> Director and Chief Medical Examiner
> North Carolina State Crime Laboratory
> Raleigh, North Carolina'"

"Tom, plans have changed. That was Tyler, and he just talked to the forensic lab. After doin' a lot of

FORENSIC REPORT

tests, they are totally sure the body that my boy, Duke, found is Stephanie's fer sure. So, we ain't gonna question Matthew when he gits here. We'll be breaking this bad news to him that the body the cops dug up was definitely his wife's. I'm gonna take a minute, call the preacher, and see if he can be with us when we break the news to Matthew 'cause he's gonna be tore slap up," Homer said.

Homer ended his call with Pastor White and said he agreed to meet them in his office.

"While we're awaitin' for Matthew and the preacher, I got somethang to say. Most of ye know that I got into this career as a detective when my half-brother got murdered a few years ago. I felt like I'd been chewed up and spit out. One of the cops took me aside and gave me some good advice that I've been able to use when I've had to tell family members that their loved one was found and had been murdered. I'll shorten this," said Homer.

Pastor White drove up and came inside. Homer asked him to have a seat.

"Today, I want ye to really watch Matthew and listen real close. Listen for any hint that Matthew might be thinking about hurtin' himself. Be patient. When my wife passed from cancer, and then when they done found my half-brother who had been shot in the head, I learnt that there are three, what they call, cycles of grief: crisis, conflict, and commencement.

"The crisis is when Stephanie disappeared, and then they found her body, made sure it was her, and now she's gonna get buried. Conflict begins with the trial and ends with the sentencing of the murderer. The commencement starts when Matthew realizes he will never see his wife again.

"So, today when we see Matthew, be careful what you say and treat him like you would like to be treated if you were in his shoes."

Chapter 7
The Investigation

There was a knock on the pastor's door, and the sheriff entered. "Hello, everyone. Pastor White asked that I join you today since I'm a law enforcement officer and a member of this church. I hope you don't mind me being here when you talk to Matthew. I've known both he and Stephanie for about eight years, so maybe I can be of help," he said. "Also, there was a reporter in my office when I got the pastor's call and since I had the phone call on speaker, unfortunately the reporter knew I was coming here."

"Well, I guess we will deal with that later. Right now, you are probably needed here. It's always a delicate situation informing family members that a loved one is a murder victim and their remains have been recovered," commented Tom.

A few minutes later, there was another knock, and Homer opened the door for Matthew. After scanning the room, Matthew said, "This is going to be bad news, isn't it?"

"Matthew, have a seat," Pastor White said as he motioned for Matthew to sit next to Homer.

"What's going on?" he asked.

"Matthew, you probably know my dog, Duke. Well, he done found a grave in the woods near that thar lake whar you done told us we ought to have a picnic. We called the cops, and they a found the body of a woman. They sent the corpse to the North Carolina State Crime Laboratory in Raleigh, where they did an autopsy," Homer told his cousin.

THE INVESTIGATION

"No! I know what you're about to say! No!" shouted Matthew.

The pastor came from around his desk and hugged Matthew who was now standing.

"Matthew, the State Lab sent their report to me today. The body was identified as Stephanie's. I'm really sorry," Homer said with tears in his eyes.

Matthew started crying and said, "No. I don't want to hear it! Who did this?"

The sheriff looked at Homer as though to get his approval to speak. Homer nodded.

"I'm sorry, Matthew, that we had to bring this news to you. I know you are hurting, but please know that we'll find the person who did this to Stephanie," the sheriff said.

After several minutes passed and Matthew was recovering from the initial shock, he asked, "Homer, what happened to her? Where is she now?"

"Watauga Medical Center," replied Homer. "The North Carolina State Crime Laboratory in Raleigh moved her here at my request. If ye want me to, I can call the funeral director and git Stephanie moved from the hospital to the funeral home."

"Yes, please," responded Matthew.

The pastor steadied Matthew with his arm and prayed, "Lord hear our cry. Please comfort Matthew and help these gentlemen find the person who killed Stephanie and bring him to justice soon! Amen." Pastor White thanked everyone for coming and said that he'd take Matthew home and stay with him awhile. He promised to call Homer later.

THE INVESTIGATION

The team walked out of the pastor's office with the sheriff, chatted briefly, shook hands, and the sheriff left.

Tom found Homer and told him that members of the press had set up outside and were asking if it was Stephanie's body that was found near Wilbur Lake. "Homer, we have to make a statement," Tom said.

"Tom, I ain't never done no press conference. Would you do it fer me?" Homer asked.

"Yes," Tom replied.

A microphone was already set up for the press conference, so Tom stationed himself in front of the reporters, picked up the microphone and began.

MURDER IN WATAUGA COUNTY

"My name is Tom Lynch with Yancey Investigative Services. We just met with Matthew Wright. Nothing we could say would ease the extreme emotional pain he is experiencing right now over the news of the death of his wife, Stephanie.

"We are hopeful that our direct and compassionate notification of her confirmed death and discovery of her body will aid in his grieving process and will bring closure for him. It was both a duty and an honor to have handled such a difficult assignment — easing the pain of a message we were entrusted to deliver.

"Mrs. Wright's remains were found near Wilbur Lake and were sent to The North Carolina State Crime

THE INVESTIGATION

Lab. The autopsy report positively identified Stephanie Wright as the murder victim.

"You can expect details regarding funeral arrangements in a few days. We respectfully request that you allow Mr. Wright his privacy as he grieves the death of his wife.

"We do not have a suspect in custody at this time, but the investigation remains active.

"Thank you for your courtesies during this difficult time," Tom concluded and walked back inside the church.

The team remained in the church hallway until all members of the press left. Homer held the door until everyone exited, but before he left the building, he saw someone out of the corner of his eye. He turned to look, and it was someone he didn't recognize. Homer extended his hand and said, "Hi, I'm Homer Yancey. Who are you?"

The shy man introduced himself as Lee Vogel and told Homer that he was the church custodian. Homer got straight to the point and asked the man if he was in the church when Stephanie was abducted. Lee told Homer he was unaware of anyone else in the church and said he was doing his routine cleaning and saw no one. Homer wrote down the man's name and phone number before leaving and then shook his hand again.

When Homer got in the car, he told everyone that they would go to the Dan'l Boone Inn Restaurant for lunch before going to the hospital to see Zach.

After placing their orders, Homer leaned in and quietly said, "Y'all, this investigation is moving 'bout as fast as a herd of turtles. We've got a few more people to interview, including Matthew, but we've gotta give him some space for a few days before we talk to him. Here's what I want us to do right now. I've got some paper and several pens," he said as he handed them out. "Okay, work with me on this. I want y'all to write down who you think has been stealin' from the church. I want you to sign it, then hand your paper to Brayden."

When the papers were collected, Homer nodded to Brayden, indicating that he read each one.

"Homer wrote Rex Smith. He is the man who scolded his wife for her shopping addiction. Tom wrote Matthew Wright."

"Brayden?" asked Homer.

"It is Leon. He is Mary Beth's husband, and he has a gambling problem."

Brayden said, "Tyler wrote Mary Beth's husband, Leon.

"Amelia?" asked Brayden.

"I think it's the pastor."

"Well, I've heard of harder to believe than that," Homer commented.

"What's the score, Brayden?" asked Homer.

"Rex, Matthew, and Pastor White each have one vote," responded Brayden. "Leon received two votes."

"Until Matthew is up to our questioning him, we'll start with Leon. Amelia, find out everythang you can on him, and after you tell us what you find out about him, we'll

THE INVESTIGATION

call him in for questioning. Okay, let's go see Zach," Homer said.

There was a tap on Victoria's hospital door. A man with a hospital name badge entered.

"Hello, Mrs. Thomas? And Mr. Thomas, I assume? I'm Lester Robinson, and I'm one of the hospital chaplains," he said as he shook their hands. "The officer standing outside your room said it was okay for me to come talk to you."

"Mrs. Thomas, I understand that a bullet from a rifle injured you, is that correct?" he asked. When she told him it was true, he said, "Well, that's the reason for my visit. Unfortunately, I've talked to several people who went through what you're experiencing right now, and as a chaplain, I wanted to come by and offer suggestions as to how you can be assured that the

Lord will see you through this. Is that okay with you, Mrs. Thomas?"

"Yes, and please call me Victoria."

After the chaplain prayed, he said, "Victoria, you may be struggling to understand how someone could shoot you and why such a terrible thing could happen. There may never be satisfactory answers to these questions. We do know, though, that it's typical for people to experience a lot of emotions after such a traumatic event.

"As I said, I've talked to several people who have been victims of a rifle wound. From what I've learned over the years, you may find trouble sleeping, concentrating, eating, or remembering even simple tasks. Don't be alarmed. These are common responses and need your rest now. Would you mind if I come back later and talk to you more about what you can experience and how you can cope?"

"Yes, of course, and you're right. I'm a bit tired right now. Do you mind if I rest?"

"Of course not. I insist," answered the chaplain.

Zach walked Chaplain Robinson into the hall. "Thank you for coming, Chaplain. Please plan to return. I think it would be good for Victoria to hear what you have to say because she's a little more frightened than she was before all this happened."

"Not a problem. Here's my card, please call me anytime. I'll come whenever needed. You be sure and take care of yourself, too, Mr. Thomas. I'm pretty sure all of this has been overwhelming for you as well.

Get some rest. I'll be back soon."

"Before you go, Chaplain, please take my business card, too. I'm Zach Thomas, the attorney for Yancey from Alabama. We're the lead team investigating the death of Stephanie Wright. I'll need to let Victoria rest now and take a few hours to meet with my boss, Homer Yancey, about the investigation."

"You may not have to take off for that. I just met Mr. Yancey in the hospital lobby, and he'll be here in just a few minutes. He seems like a very caring person. I'll leave so you can visit with him. Thank you for your business card. My advice to you right now is not to try to skip meals. If you start skipping meals, you'll not be as alert as you need to be."

"Of course, you're right. Thank you for reminding me. I need to be at my best for Victoria. Chaplain, I haven't eaten today," said Zach.

Just as he made that comment, Homer and the team walked towards him with a carry-out bag from the restaurant where they had lunch.

"Now that's what I call good timing," Zach said with a laugh.

"What's got you tickled?" asked Homer.

"Nothing worth pursuing," laughed Zach. "I sure hope that bag of food is for me. I haven't eaten all day and I'm hungry." As Homer handed him the sack of food, Lester Robinson introduced himself, shook hands and then excused himself so Homer and Zach could visit.

"How's your sweetie, Zach?" asked Homer.

"Dr. Smith said she's recovering just as he had hoped. He said that she's young, in good health otherwise, and she's a fighter. Those are indicators that she'll recover. I really like him. He said that tomorrow Victoria will move from SICU into a private room because she is doing so well. I'm grateful Dr. Smith is her doctor because I think he's providing good healthcare and has a good sense of humor," commented Zach. "Homer, thanks for being my friend through all this. It means a lot. Even though my family is here, I am grateful for your presence."

"Take that sack of food ye got in your hand, Zach. Friends buy you food, best friends eat your food," Homer said as he grabbed the sack out of Zach's hand and ran laughing towards the elevator.

Zach outran him.

THE INVESTIGATION

When Homer got off the elevator on the first floor, he walked over to Tom.

"Homer, Leon has agreed to come to the church for questioning. We have just enough time to get to the church before he arrives."

When Leon arrived, he was met by Tom, Homer, and Amelia.

"What's this all about?" Leon asked when he recognized Homer from his picture in the newspaper.

"Have a seat, please. Do you mind if we call you Leon?" asked Tom as he extended his hand. "I'm Tom Lynch and this is Homer Yancey. We're with Yancey and we have been asked to head the murder investigation of Stephanie Wright. Today, we have a few questions we'd like to ask you."

"I didn't kill Stephanie! Is that what you think?"

"Calm down, Leon. No one is saying you killed her. We're just trying to git some answers so we can put the sleaze bag in the slammer," said Homer in a reassuring tone.

"Stephanie was my wife's friend, not mine, so why am I here?" asked Leon.

"I'm glad you asked that. You see, we have reason to believe that someone has been stealing from the church and your name appeared in Stephanie's logbook. In the entry, your wife told her you had a gambling problem. Do you have a gambling problem, Leon?"

"Well, yes, I do, but I didn't kill Stephanie over it."

THE INVESTIGATION

"We understand you have a debt of $34,000. That is enough money to cause someone to do something illegal to get the money to pay the debt off," Tom said.

"Hey, don't write something into this. Yes, I do owe money, but I've taken on a second job to earn money to pay off the debt. That can be verified," Leon said in a nervous tone.

"Where you workin' at?" asked Homer.

"I took a second job on the weekends with Bar-b-que Bob's. I drive a delivery truck. Mr. Yancey, I didn't kill Stephanie!"

"I believe ye, Leon. Ye can go now, but we might be callin' ye later." instructed Homer.

The men shook hands as Leon left the pastor's office.

Homer started pacing and scratching his head. Tom left him alone to finish his thinking. A few minutes later, Homer said, "It's 'bout time we git Matthew to come in to ask him some questions. I'll give him a call and we'll just git it over with. Because I'm close to him, you need to ask the questions. Are you okay with that, Tom?"

"Sure. I agree that I should be the one asking the questions. Call him, Homer." Tom said.

Homer reached into his back pocket, pulled out his cell phone, briefly stared at it and then keyed in Matthew's number.

"Matthew, this is Homer. Me and Tom are in the preacher's office trying to put the pieces together in Stephanie's case and we are puzzled about a few things and think ye might be able to help us figger it out. Could you spare some time and come down here right now? It's important."

"Yeah, sure. I'll be right there. See you in a minute."

"Tom, he's coming right away."

Matthew arrived within thirty minutes of Homer's call.

"Hi guys, what's up?" Matthew said as he entered the pastor's office.

"To be honest, Matthew, we feel like we ain't gittin' any closer to findin' out who done killed Stephanie. We figgered you might could help us. We have a few thangs to ask you," answered Homer.

"Am I a suspect, Homer?"

"I just said we've gotta few questions, Matthew."

Tom quickly took over. "Matthew, do you know of anyone who was threatening Stephanie?"

"If there was someone, she never mentioned it to me, so, no, I don't think so," replied Matthew.

"I know you've had a lot of time to think about this. Who do you think could've done this?" Tom asked.

"You're right, I've done a lot of thinking about this. I honestly don't know who could've done this. I do know that as church administrator, she talked to a lot of street people who came to the church wanting gas money, groceries, and other supplies. I didn't know many of them. She was such a loving and sincere person, I can't imagine anyone taking her life.

THE INVESTIGATION

"Do you know who Stephanie was with shortly before she was killed?" Homer asked.

"No, I don't. That was the first question I asked Pastor White the night she disappeared. He didn't know either."

"Where were you when Stephanie was killed?" Tom asked.

"You asked me that when I hired your firm," an irritated Matthew answered.

"Please, Matthew, don't be mad, just answer the question," interrupted Homer.

"The Dan 'l Boone Inn Restaurant where we met every Thursday night for a date," replied Matthew.

"When did you last see her alive?" asked Tom.

"When I left for work."

"Is there anything you remember about the day she disappeared that you haven't told us?" asked Tom.

"Nothing. Sorry."

"We understand that you and Stephanie had planned and saved for an anniversary trip to Scotland and Ireland. Want to tell us why you used those savings to buy your pickup truck instead? What was your plan to pay the money back?" asked Tom.

A very frightened and nervous Matthew hung his head and asked, "How in the world did you know that? Stephanie couldn't have told you!"

"So, it is true?" asked Homer.

THE INVESTIGATION

"Yeah, I'm embarrassed to say, it's true. I did use the money for my truck, and I did promise to pay it back. She was pretty upset. I don't know why I did such a selfish thing to the woman I loved."

"Matthew, we don't have any more questions currently, and we appreciate you coming to talk to us. Please know that we're going to find who murdered your wife. Hopefully all this will be behind us very soon," assured Tom.

Matthew stood, shook hands with everyone and left.

Chapter 8
Investigative Detention

"Don't worry y'all, I got it all. I made notes on my computer. I'll type it up and print you a copy," Amelia said as soon as Matthew closed the door.

"Homer, I don't want to stick my nose in where it doesn't belong, but I was wondering if we should interview the pastor, nearby neighbors, or even the custodian?" suggested Amelia.

"You're catching on, young lady! Now you're thinking like a team member. You've just made a great suggestion." Homer said smiling.

"When we get back to the cabin, our man Tyler can set those interviews up. He needs to call Detective Adamson and git any notes on people he done already interviewed. I don't think the sheriff interviewed nobody but Matthew and Pastor White so thar ain't no reason to call him," Homer added.

It was a short drive back to the cabin. "Everybody, I'd like for y'all to meet in the living room in 'bout an hour. We gotta talk about this case and figure out why we ain't moving forward with the right suspect. Bring your notepads," Homer instructed.

An hour later, Tom, Tyler, Brayden, Zach, and Amelia were exchanging small talk while waiting on Homer. He appeared and glanced around the room and did a double-take when he saw Zach.

"What are you doing here? Shouldn't you be at the hospital with Victoria?"

A voice from behind Homer asked, "Why, when I'm right here?"

INVESTIGATIVE DETENTION

"Victoria! Are you doin' okay? Aren't you home too early? Can I get you somethang? Don't you need to be in bed? Are you hungry?" Homer asked with concerned excitement.

After the laughter stopped, Victoria explained that her doctor said she could go home with bed rest, and she assured Homer that she intended to do just that.

"Let me give ye a hug." said Homer.

"Of course, then I do think I'll rest some while the greatest investigators on earth do their job," Victoria said as Zach stood, took her by the arm, and helped her to their room.

Homer started the discussion by asking, "What did y'all git from Matthew's interview today?"

Amelia was first to answer. "He was unusually nervous considering his wife has been dead for at least six weeks. I know her death wasn't confirmed until recently, but she has been gone for six weeks. What exactly was there for him to be so nervous about?

"Well, I'll be dad gum, Amelia. That's good," said Homer.

"Tom, since you're the teacher, why don't you answer her questions?"

"Glad to, Homer. The way police work in the event of a homicide is to start with the immediate family and the spouse or significant other and work outward from there. So, the people in the inner circle are investigated first. They are questioned and their whereabouts checked to see if they were at or near the scene of the murder when it occurred. Also, a very large percentage of women who are murdered are killed by their husbands or their partners. **Statistically, the most likely to have committed the crime is either the closest person to the victim or someone who hated them."**

"Brayden, I think Matthew's story sounds a little fishy. He told us that he and Stephanie had a date every Thursday night at the **Daniel Boone Restaurant at 6:00** p.m., but he didn't call her or even go to the church 'til thirty minutes or so later. He done thought she weren't coming or forgot 'bout him. He sounded to me like he was gittin' mad 'cause he said he went to the church to check on her and to listen to her excuse.

"**Brayden,** I want ye to go to the Dan' l Boone Restaurant around suppertime and ask the workers if they done seen Matthew the night Stephanie was murdered. Also, ask the Boone Police Department and the Watauga Sheriff's Department if they know anything 'bout Matthew going to the spot where Duke found Stephanie's body," Homer instructed.

"Tyler, after we're done eatin' supper tonight, I want you to bring us up to date on the church audit," Homer said.

"One more thang, I want everybody to help Victoria. She needs to git stronger and git well. I'm pretty sure the bullet that hit Victoria really had my name on it. Tom, you and Zach stay on this. Don't let it git cold. We need to find out whodunit before somebody else gits hurt. Update us tonight," Homer said as he looked over at Tom.

"Thanks, Homer, I've got it covered!" replied Tom.

Homer cleared his throat before saying, "I'll be at the church all day tomorrow."

INVESTIGATIVE DETENTION

"One more thing since we're still together. Victoria's been fixin' our meals. We're all goin' to be busy, but we do like to stop to eat." Everyone laughed.

"Zach and I'll take care of it, Homer. Before our team got this big, we were the cooks. We'll be glad to do it again. I'll tell him and I'm sure he'll be all in!"

"Thanks, Tyler! Here's my credit card," Homer said. "Okay, any questions or suggestions? No? Then let's git 'er done.

"Brayden, call the car rental place and git them to bring us five cars. We're all gonna be goin' different places tomorrow and we just got one. Brayden, stick with one type of car, but different colors, and don't order the priciest ones they got on the dad blame lot. Why don't ye call right now and see when they can bring 'em over? We'll drink some more coffee while you call," Homer ordered.

"Come on, Duke, let's take a walk."

Homer did his best thinking while walking with Duke beside the Watauga River.

"We need to talk to Matthew some more," he thought to himself as he was mentally struggling with what he really should do. He was leaning towards having Matthew placed under investigative detention, so he could be interrogated.

"I can't have my blood kin locked up, even for 24 hours! His wife was murdered, and we think he might have done it. Lord, help me make the right decision." He thought to himself, then said aloud, "Duke, let's get back inside and talk to Tom about this."

INVESTIGATIVE DETENTION

Since he had been deep in thought, Homer had walked more than three quarters of a mile with Duke and then that amount back to the cabin. Realizing this, he said, "Whew! I ain't no young fella no more, Duke. Let's not go so far next time." After petting Duke, he looked up and saw five cars parked in front of the cabin. They were all SUVs.

"Good job, Brayden. Which one did ye git me?" asked Homer.

"The black one. It's the only one that is a Mercedes. It was made in Alabama. The others are all Ford Explorer's. Here are your keys, Homer," Brayden said.

"Thanks, Brayden. Make sure you done made a list of who will git a car, the color of that car, and maybe even their cell phone number. Hang this information in the kitchen so everybody can see it," instructed Homer.

"Actually, Homer, I've already done just that," he said laughing.

"That don't surprise me none!!"

"Give me a minute, Brayden, I need to talk to Tom." The two men stepped aside, and Homer started talking in a whisper. "Whatcha think about interrogating Matthew?"

"We need enough on him to be a suspect to do that," Tom responded.

"What did Brayden find out today?" asked Homer.

During supper, the team gave reports. It was Brayden's turn.

INVESTIGATIVE DETENTION

"I went to the Dan'l Boone Restaurant about thirty minutes ago and talked to several servers. They said that Matthew didn't go to the restaurant the night that Stephanie was murdered. They all thought it was strange for Matthew not to be at the restaurant since he and Stephanie met there every Thursday night.

"I also went to the police department and spoke with Chief Daniel Cornelius. He said that when he arrived at the church the night Stephanie disappeared, he, the pastor, and Matthew went to Stephanie's office. He did notice that the room was in disarray, and it was obvious she had been hard at work that day, but her trash can was empty. He said that there was a spilled drink on her desk and the floor and he thought it was strange that her purse was not in her office. It was possible she took it with her, but because her office was in disarray, he felt like she left in a hurry. He doubted she would have grabbed her purse before leaving.

"The chief said that after Matthew left, he asked the pastor a few questions. He wanted to know if Matthew and Stephanie seemed to be getting along and in his opinion were they happy together. The pastor assured the chief they were definitely a happy couple.

"The chief apologized and said that in all the commotion since we arrived, he had neglected to turn over his notes. He found them on his messy desk at the police department and gave them to me to give to you. The chief said that he thinks it might be a good idea to interrogate Matthew.

"Neither the sheriff nor the chief said they have any

INVESTIGATIVE DETENTION

proof that Matthew went to the site where Stephanie's remains were found."

Homer grabbed his phone and called Chief Deputy Steven Adamson. "Deputy Adamson, this is Homer Yancey. How are ye doin' tonight? You're working late, and so are we. I'm calling 'cause we think we need to interrogate Matthew Wright. What do we need to do to make that happen?" Homer asked as he pressed the speaker function on his phone so the team could hear.

"We can bring him in and can legally hold him for 48-hours on what is called an investigative detention," Steven said.

"Steven, this is Tyler Frye. What exactly is an investigative detention?"

"It's a temporary seizure of a suspect for the purpose of determining, (1) whether there is probable cause to arrest him, (2) whether further investigation is necessary, or (3) whether the officer's suspicions were unfounded."

"Go ahead and do it. Let me know when he's in your custody," said Homer and he ended the call.

Homer was quiet for a few minutes before he told the team about what was going to happen to Matthew. "I was hoping we wouldn't have to do this. But it's not my job to let my feelings git in the way of this investigation, so we're gonna interrogate Matthew. So far, we ain't got no suspect."

"I think we need to continue our questioning of several people, including the pastor, nearby neighbors and the custodian as was suggested tonight," said Tyler. "Do you want me to set up those interviews, Homer?"

"Sure, we gotta try somethang 'cause so far he's the only suspect we got," responded Homer. "As soon as Matthew is behind bars, we can have more interviews.

"We must git our questions wrote down fer Matthew. You, Brayden, and Zach get your notepads and take the questions down that we decide on," instructed Homer.

"Zach, you, and Amelia contact the funeral home and tell 'em we are investigating the murder of Stephanie Wright. We wanna know who the insurance company was who paid fer her funeral. Once you get that information, contact the company and find out the amount of her policy. If they refuse to provide that information, we can get Steven to have the information subpoenaed. Being the beneficiary of a large insurance policy could be the motive behind taking someone's life," Homer said.

"Homer, that's really good thinking!" commented Tom.

"We'll get right on that, Homer. Before we get started, I have a question. Does Matthew have to be read his Miranda rights if he is in investigative detention?" asked Tyler. "And I have two more questions. Who is 'Miranda,' and why are the rights named after her?'"

"It's real good that we got Tom on our team. As you know, he used to be a teacher of this stuff. So, Tom, would you tell us what you know 'bout this?" Homer asked.

"I'll be glad to, Homer," replied Tom. "Anyone who has watched a television show about law enforcement has heard a police officer read the suspect his or her Miranda Rights. After placing the suspect under arrest, the officer will say something like, 'You have the right to remain silent. Anything you say can and will be used against you in a court of law. You have a right to an attorney. If you cannot afford an attorney, one will be appointed for you.' The wording of the Miranda rights may be different from what I just said, but if they fully convey the message, then it is okay. The officer must also make sure that the suspect understands his or her rights. If, for example, the suspect does not speak English, these rights must be translated to make sure they're understood.

"To answer one of your questions, Miranda isn't a female. In 1966, there was a case before the United States Supreme Court. The case is known as Miranda v. Arizona. Ernesto Morando was the suspect. The Miranda warning is intended to protect the suspect's Fifth Amendment right to refuse to answer self-incriminating questions.

"Tyler, you should write this down. It's important to note that Miranda rights don't go into effect until and if Matthew is arrested. We're free to ask questions while he's in investigative detention, but it's not necessary to read him his rights. Even though he is not read his rights, everything he says or does can be used against him in a court of law. "Another important fact to jot down, Tyler, is that silence can be used against Matthew if he chooses to go that route before he is read the Miranda rights. The prosecution will try to use Matthew's silence against him in court.

"Naturally, we can't tell Matthew this because we're the ones trying to get him to confess. Since he's being investigated for his wife's murder and he chooses to remain silent before being Mirandized, he can inform us that his attorney told him to never answer questions without talking to him first. This looks less suspicious than simply refusing to answer questions.

"I hope answering your questions didn't take too long, Tyler. I didn't see you nod off, so I guess I wasn't boring. Hopefully, my answer helps you better understand the Miranda rights."

"Just to put it another way, here's what really happens, Tyler," Homer said. "If you're really a suspect and we've got enough on ye fer ye to get arrested after we done asked ye questions, but you refuse to go in so we can pick your brain some more, this is what's gonna happen. Ye may as well put your hands behind your back … because ye <u>are</u> gonna go in for questioning." That comment got plenty of laughter.

"Brayden, ye, and Amelia git in touch with Chief Deputy Sheriff Adamson and tell him that since Matthew will be brought in for interrogation, it would a great learning experience for you and Amelia if he would grant you permission to observe the entire process," Homer instructed.

Early the next day, Watauga County Chief Deputy Sheriff Steven Adamson and two other sheriff deputies arrived at Matthew's house and informed him that he was under arrest and was being brought in for interrogation regarding the murder of his wife Stephanie Wright. He would be held under what is called an investigative hold for 48 hours.

Matthew told Deputy Adamson that he'd cooperate and go peacefully with him. He just wanted to put his shoes on, so the deputy allowed it. Since he was an investigator

INVESTIGATIVE DETENTION

for the department, Deputy Adamson followed Matthew into his bedroom and scanned the room while Matthew put on his shoes. The other deputies walked from room to room scanning for weapons and other incriminating evidence. Usually officers do this as a "free inspection" prior to getting a search warrant.

Matthew was then handcuffed and placed in the patrol car.

Once at the Watauga County Sheriff's Department, he was brought into the interrogation room where Homer and his team were waiting.

Right off the bat, Homer asked, "Matthew, you're a little shy on answers. Ye got anythang else to say?"

Chapter 9
To the Woodshed

"You know, Homer, I don't think I want to do that without having my lawyer with me. Even if while meeting with you I proclaimed my innocence, without a lawyer, there's a chance I may say something that you think makes me a suspect.

"This may sound silly, Homer, but I have watched enough police television shows to know that you guys are masters at getting people to admit things and spotting lies or inconsistencies. You'll ask the same question, repeatedly, in different ways, then point out small differences to my answers. Then you'll use the inconsistencies to question the validity of my entire statement. So, no, I'll not answer any questions without my lawyer. He can prevent this from happening by making sure

I understand the question I'm being asked, and by making sure I don't say more than what you're seeking.

"Homer, you may be my cousin, and I know you're a famous detective, but I can't even imagine why you'd want me to come back in for more questioning. For heaven's sake, Homer! I just buried the woman I love who was murdered and snatched away from me, and you have the nerve to even possibly think that I did it? My attorney, who believes in my innocence, will be with me during questioning.

Homer just stood there staring at Matthew. Tom took him by the arm which jolted Homer back to his job at hand. As Homer and Tom were walking away, Homer said, "I'm gonna tell him I'm sorry, Tom. He's right. I don't know if he done it or not, but I do remember how I felt when I buried my wife. Maybe I need to quit thinkin' like a detective at a time like this and be nicer."

An hour later, a tall man dressed in a business suit stood at the front desk and identified himself as William **J**. Miller, the attorney for Matthew Wright.

After Mr. Miller signed in and his credentials were approved, the receiving deputy called Homer to inform him that Matthew's attorney had arrived. Another deputy escorted Mr. Miller to the interrogation room on the second floor where he was greeted by Brayden, Amelia, and Matthew. Brayden and Amelia left Matthew and his attorney alone and waited outside the door for Homer.

Twenty minutes later, Homer, Tom, Brayden, Amelia, and Tyler entered the room. After the proper introductions, a calmer Homer said, "Sorry we done had to bring ye in this way, Matthew, but this here's the legal way the State's got fer us to keep on asking ye questions. We didn't bring ye in to point the finger, but to talk some more.

"To be frank, we do have a couple of things we need you to clear up fer us. First, ye told us that the night Stephanie disappeared, ye were at the Dan' l Boone Restaurant waitin' fer her to git thar fer your regular Thursday night date.

"Am I right 'bout that, Matthew?" asked Homer.

Matthew looked at his attorney with a frightened expression.

Mr. Miller said, "I'd like to confer with my client."

He and Matthew stood by the door and talked for a few minutes, then were seated again.

TO THE WOODSHED

Matthew spoke, his voice shaking. "Homer, I don't have an excuse why I told you that, because it's not true. I didn't go to the restaurant because I went to pick up a bracelet for Stephanie at the jeweler. I had it engraved and was going to give it to her that night. There was no reason for the gift other than my apology for using our trip money to buy my pickup truck."

"I wanta see the bracelet you're claimin' ye bought, Matthew, and the receipt fer the engraving. Your lawyer or one of his guys can bring it to me," said Homer.

"Is that all, Homer?" asked Matthew.

"I'm afraid not. Did you go in Stephanie's office and empty the garbage can before the cops came?"

Again, Matthew had a frightened look on his face.

"And did ye take Stephanie's pocketbook?"

Matthew had tears in his eyes as he looked at his attorney.

Mr. Miller instructed Matthew to answer the questions.

"Yes, I emptied the garbage can and I took Stephanie's pocketbook and put it in my car. I didn't want people going through her personal belongings," answered Matthew.

Tom interrupted, "Matthew, why did you do that? You need to consult your attorney, because I'm sure he knows that tampering with physical evidence carries a heavy punishment."

Tom leaned in as he said, "We can charge you with obstruction of justice because you tampered with evidence and you lied to us. North Carolina punishes obstruction of justice as a felony with penalties of up to three years in prison. You may want to talk to Mr. Miller right now. You'll be spending the night in a holding cell sleeping on a mat on the cold floor. You'll be all alone, which should give you some soul-searching time to think about everything, but in the morning, we want answers!" Tom said, then motioned for the team to leave.

On the way out of the building, Homer told the sheriff they'd be back in the morning to continue Matthew's interrogation.

When they got back to the cabin, Homer's cell phone rang. "Hey, this is Homer."

"Matthew didn't do it," a man's voice said. The line went dead.

Homer looked at his phone and called the number displayed by caller ID. He heard a message stating the number was no longer in service.

Homer looked at Tom and asked, "The number don't work. Can the police trace it anyhow?"

"Why do you ask?"

After Homer told everyone of his mysterious phone call, he turned to Tom and repeated his question.

Tom scratched his head, took a deep breath, and then said, "A cell phone still communicates with nearby towers even if it's disconnected, but the exact registration identification of the device can't be determined in a disconnected state. In other words, authorities would simply be 'chasing a ghost' without having the key identifiers of the device itself."

TO THE WOODSHED

"Dad blast it!" Homer shouted.

"It was a man on the phone, but I don't know who. Now how in blazes could he know that we just talked to Matthew?" Homer said as he was thinking aloud.

"He didn't know. The phone call could have just been unusual timing. We could leave it at that and not go down that road as they say," commented Zach.

"I guess. I'm just gittin' the heebie jeebies," Homer replied.

"How do we manage that phone call, Homer?" asked Tyler. "Do we need to call the sheriff and let him know?"

"No, we're the guys in charge. We're gonna look under every rock and if we need the sheriff, we'll call him. Whatcha think 'bout that, Tom?"

"Definitely."

"Now, let's git back on track. We ain't found the gun used on Stephanie. Don't ye think we should get a search warrant and see if we find it at Matthew's place?" asked Homer.

"Yes, every rock uncovered," said Zach, who had just entered the room.

"Hey, man! How's Victoria?" asked Homer.

"She's getting stronger every day and she's thankful to be here with everybody. She plans to join us for breakfast in the morning, then her parents are coming over to stay with her so I can go with you to the jail," said Zach smiling.

TO THE WOODSHED

"Homer, I have a request. Before I tell you what it is, I want you to know that I will not be offended if you say 'no,'" Zach said reassuringly.

"We have a couple of spare rooms here in the cabin. Would you mind allowing Victoria's parents to use one of the rooms? Victoria's mom is a really good cook and I'm sure she would love to help that way, and also look after Victoria so I can continue working.'" Zach said.

"Son, you musta took a law course on persuasion, and made a durn good grade, 'cause you done presented a good case and won!" Homer said grinning. "Tell 'em we are happy they'll be right here to help."

Homer's reply got a hug from Zach.

The team went into the living room and spent a few minutes updating Zach on the latest developments with Matthew. Then Zach picked up where he left off.

"We can't get a search warrant here in North Carolina because only a law enforcement officer can apply and do the searching," Zach informed the team.

"No problem, we'll just tell the chief deputy sheriff tomorrow that we'd like for Matthew's house to be searched for the gun, and let him manage it for us," commented Tyler.

"Sounds like a plan. Let's get some shuteye. We gotta big day tomorrow," said Homer.

In the meantime, at the jail, when he was certain no one was looking, a law enforcement officer grabbed a key to Matthew's cell. He then walked down the hallway to the fourth cell and looked at his watch. It was 2:00 a.m. He turned the lock and switched on the light. It startled Matthew and he asked what time it was. The deputy told him it was 2:00 a.m.

"What's going on?" Matthew asked.

The officer reached into his pocket and produced an evidence bag which held a gun and a silencer. Wearing gloves, he handed Matthew the gun with the silencer attached and asked, "Have you ever seen these items, Matthew?"

Matthew held the gun and silencer and then quickly handed it back with tears in his eyes. "Is this the gun that killed Stephanie?" he asked.

"So, this IS the gun you used the night you shot and killed your wife?" the officer asked.

"No!"

"Goodnight, Matthew. I hope you do some soul searching tonight and decide to come clean tomorrow," the officer said as he turned out the lights and locked the cell door.

Since this was not the officer's regular shift, he quickly entered the empty central office and switched on the surveillance camera for Matthew's cell. He placed the evidence bag with the gun and silencer in his jacket, then walked into the room where several deputies were working.

He said, "Hey, I just noticed that the camera in Matthew Wright's holding cell wasn't on. Let's get sharp, guys! We were told to observe him. I noticed it and turned it on. I'm going home. Let the sheriff know if Mr. Wright does anything unusual."

TO THE WOODSHED

He told everyone goodnight, then walked to the rear of the building and exited.

Someone was waiting for him outside. "Did you get his prints?" he asked.

"I did. Now, am I going to be cleared of the violations against me? I need to make sergeant," he pleaded.

"I'll talk to the higher ups in the morning. You have my word," he said, and they both left.

The next morning, Homer and the team purposely started late to make Matthew nervous. When they entered the interrogation room, Matthew and his lawyer were already there discussing his options.

The interrogation lasted about two hours before they stopped for lunch. Matthew was taken back to the holding area and the lawyer agreed to meet again with the investigators at 2:00 p.m.

The team went to the Dan'l Boone Restaurant. Homer was unusually quiet even when he was bombarded with questions from team members. He did not seem interested in eating, either. It was noticeable to everyone, so finally Zach asked, "Homer, what is on your mind? Is everything okay?"

Homer did not look up or answer. He just kept playing with the food on his plate.

Tom, who was seated next to Homer, stood, took Homer by the arm, and said, "Come with me," while practically pulling him.

Homer was bumfuzzled but snapped out of his fog and asked, "Where we headed to?"

TO THE WOODSHED

Tom replied, "To the woodshed!"

Once outside, Tom said, "Alright, Homer. What is with you?"

"I just don't think my cuz killed his wife."

"Then prove that he didn't! Now let's go eat," Tom said. He went back inside alone.

Homer paced back and forth on the sidewalk. He looked straight up and said, "Lord, if ye can hear me, I need ye to help me. I need a clue 'bout whodunit." He went back in, sat down, and devoured his lunch.

"Okay team, listen up. Now that we've got Matthew in investigative detention, the clock's a tickin.' We've only got him for 48 hours. We need to search his house for evidence since so far in this case, we ain't got no proof he killed Stephanie.

"After lunch, we'll go back to the sheriff's department and talk to him some more. I'm startin' to doubt that Matthew is going to confess. I'm gonna ask the chief deputy sheriff to go to the magistrate and git us a search warrant of Matthew's place.

"I asked Amelia to find out how we can git a search warrant in Boone. Amelia, tell us whatcha learnt," commented Homer.

"In North Carolina, a magistrate will issue a search warrant based on evidence compiled and presented by law enforcement. They must show probable cause or have a reasonable belief that Matthew committed a crime or participated in criminal activity to obtain a search warrant of his house.

TO THE WOODSHED

"The search warrant must specify the areas of the home to be searched. Any evidence discovered during a lawful search can be used against Matthew to charge him with the crime," explained Amelia.

"Looks like our task today is to get Deputy Adamson to ask the magistrate to sign off on a search warrant. I wonder if we can just say the entire premises including the garage, basement, and car?" asked Zach.

"Good thinkin', Zach," Homer said. "Let's start out with that and if that don't work, we'll go with plan B."

When they got back to the sheriff's department, Homer asked Chief Deputy Sheriff Adamson to help them get a search warrant. "If the magistrate says okay, we want to search Matthew's whole place."

Chief Deputy Adamson looked pleased and told Homer he would make the request right away. Around 3:00 p.m. Chief Deputy Adamson came into the interrogation room and asked Homer to step into the hallway.

"Homer, the magistrate has approved our request for a search warrant. It was issued about thirty minutes ago. I told the sheriff that we obtained the search warrant and he suggested we leave in about an hour. So, you need to decide who on your team will be going to Mr. Wright's house. Instruct them to bring a notebook and their phones in order to take pictures, if needed. You can continue your questioning of Mr. Wright and I'll get you around 4:00 p.m."

"Thanks, Steven," responded Homer. Steven smiled because it was the first time that Homer called him by his first name.

TO THE WOODSHED

Homer went back into the interrogation room and told Matthew that their request for a search warrant had been approved, and they would be searching his property for evidence.

"Before we go to your house, is there anythang you need to tell us before we start searchin'?" Homer asked.

"Like, did I kill my wife?" asked Matthew. "The answer is still NO!"

"By the way, Matthew, I asked you to bring me the bracelet ye said ye bought Stephanie the day she was murdered and the receipt for it. Did ye have your lawyer bring 'em thangs?" asked Homer.

Matthew's attorney, Mr. Miller, reached into his coat pocket and produced the bracelet and the receipt. He handed the items to Homer.

While the interrogation continued, a law enforcement officer arrived at Matthew's house and went inside briefly. In less than ten minutes, the officer came outside, got in his cruiser, and drove back to the department.

At 4:00 p.m., Steven tapped on the interrogation room door, stepped inside and then said, "Let's go, guys."

Chapter 10
The Arrest

Matthew was placed back in his holding cell. Homer, Tom, and Tyler rode together. Five sheriff deputies carrying additional officers came also. The sheriff and Steven rode together.

It was a beautiful, clear day in Matthew's neighborhood. People were working in their yards, planting flowers, cutting grass, and trimming hedges. When the Watauga County Sheriff's Department vehicles slowly drove into the Whispering Woods subdivision and parked in front of Matthew's house, it created quite a commotion. The officers saw the reaction their presence created, but they had a job to do. At least a dozen deputies either went inside the house or searched the garage, backyard, storage buildings, and the woods next to Matthew's property line.

The deputies who were inside began their search. Homer, Tom, and Steven stayed together, and others paired off as well. Steven suggested that the three of them take a room each then meet to discuss their findings. Homer began in Matthew's bedroom.

"I really don't like going through my cousin's stuff, but I guess I gotta do my job," Homer said to himself.

He began his search in the closet. "I'll bet Stephanie kept this here closet more cleaner than this. It's kinda sad to see her clothes and stuff jest like as she likely left 'em. I guess I did the same thang when my darlin' wife passed. Well, nuttin' unusual in here. I reckon I'll look in the chester drawers. Nuttin' unusual here either." Homer said.

Finding nothing of interest, his attention turned to the nightstand. Homer opened the top drawer.

THE ARREST

"Well, well, what do my eyes behold here?" Homer asked himself.

"Tom, Steven, y'all need to come into Matthew's bedroom rite now!" Homer said loud enough for them to hear. When the two men walked into the room, they saw Homer, with a sad look on his face as he pointed to the open nightstand drawer. As Tom and Steven approached Homer, they saw a small caliber pistol with an attached silencer in the drawer.

"This is huge, Homer, and you're incredible!" commented Tom.

Steven immediately found the sheriff and informed him that the gun and silencer had been located.

The sheriff spoke loud enough for his deputies to hear him say, "Okay everyone, while searching Mr.

Wright's bedroom, Homer found a small caliber revolver and silencer! We will be sending them to forensics to determine if they were used in Mrs. Wright's murder. Stay alert, team. There could be more evidence to uncover here."

After a few more hours of probing without additional evidence found, the sheriff called off the search.

The deputies congratulated Homer for finding possible major evidence. Sheriff Reed shook Homer's hand and said, "You're a dang good detective!"

The sheriff turned to Steven and instructed him to send the gun and silencer to forensics for prints. "Tell them we are requesting they conduct tests to determine if the bullet which entered Stephanie's temple was fired from this gun. Request they send their report ASAP."

Steven responded, "Yes sir."

THE ARREST

When they returned to the sheriff's department, the team met in the interrogation room. Homer spoke first, "Y'all know I have felt all along that Matthew didn't murder his wife. For those of ye who didn't go with us to Matthew's house today, ye should know that a gun and silencer were found and have been sent to forensics. They will do analysis of the weapon and the bullet retrieved at the gravesite. What we now have is … what did ye call it Tom? Oh yeah, I remember. It is 'associative evidence.' Tom said it means that this evidence could connect Matthew to the crime.

"Yancey Investigative Services ain't done. We've got more folks to talk to, and we ain't gotta copy of that final forensic report with photos, like Dr. Macy McElderry promised. In case ye don't remember, this is the forensic testin' of Stephanie's body when they found her.

"And we ain't found out if thar's some connection between her murder and the attempted murder of Victoria. Have I forgotten anything?" Homer asked.

Zach spoke up, "We haven't heard from Mr. Cleveland with Forensic Accounting Services in Asheville about whether or not someone was stealing money from the church."

Brayden added, "We haven't tried to see if we can determine what was written on the page that Stephanie tore from her logbook."

Homer broke in and said, "It sounds like I need to tell y'all some things to do to git ye started.

"Tyler, since you were the one to deal with Dr. McElderry the first time, ye can ask him to give us a full report with pictures.

THE ARREST

"Zach, call Mr. Cleveland and tell him we want a full report from his company 'bout what they done found out 'bout whoever done stole from the Hickory Grove Baptist Church. As soon as ye git that report, let me know and ye can read it to our team," Homer instructed.

"Since it is already past 6:00 p.m., I'll call them first thing in the morning, and if the report is ready, I'll ask them to fax it to me," Zach responded. "Better still, I have Mr. Cleveland's business card here in my pocket," he said as he searched pocket after pocket until he found it. "I'll just email him tonight."

Duke greeted everyone as they entered the cabin. He was petted until satisfied that everyone was accounted for, then went to his "daytime" bed in the corner.

"Duke has been restless all day. I think he wants to be more a part of the team," laughed Mrs. Owen.

|221|

"Zach, I can honestly tell you that I think Victoria is improving. She has a doctor's appointment in the morning and her father and I want to take her. Is that okay with you? We promise to give you a full report."

"That would be appreciated. I have plenty to do with a team assignment and knowing that someone is taking care of my sweetheart takes worry off my back," responded Zach.

"Speaking of an assignment, I'm going to slip away for a minute and send an email. I'll rejoin everyone for dinner."

When Zach returned to the dining room, Victoria caught his eye. She was holding two full dinner plates. She motioned for Zach to get the utensils and drinks and they disappeared onto the porch.

THE ARREST

Brayden, who had seen them leave, said, "Ain't love grand?"

Everyone laughed and then continued eating and having fun together. Homer glanced over at Tom, smiled, and gave a thumbs up. Tom returned the smile.

Around 8:30 p.m., Zach and Victoria went to their room. A few minutes later, Zach emerged carrying a document. After getting everyone's attention, he said, "I decided to check my email and I got a response from Mr. Cleveland with the Forensic Auditors. Homer, would you like for me to read his report? It's brief."

"Yes! Let's have it!" replied Homer.

"Hickory Grove Baptist Church, a faith-based organization, embraces trust and forgiveness. While these are very important and admirable core values, it is the opinion of Forensic Accounting Services, that this is what left the organization at risk for theft.

Unfortunately, the church's mission statement alone did not sufficiently protect it from violations of trust. The reality is that the faith of Hickory Grove Baptist Church created a culture of unquestioned trust in its members. This put the organization at risk for breaches of trust that resulted in stealing from the offering and alms boxes without fear of punishment.

In this case, prints were lifted from inside the offering and alms boxes in the back of the church. It was determined that the perpetrator is Rex Smith. According to Yancey Investigative Services' notes of the interview with Mr. Smith, he told his wife that he would do whatever it took (rationalization) to get the needed funds to fix their financial problem (incentive). Based on the previous deposits made within the last **three** years from tithes, offerings, and designated offerings, it is estimated that the amount of theft is approximately $17,000."

Gary Cleveland, President
Cleveland Accounting Services
Asheville, North Carolina

"Wow! That's interesting! I think we need to tell Chief Deputy Adamson as soon as possible, because Mr. Smith needs to be arrested, don't you agree?" Tyler asked.

THE ARREST

"I think it would be okay to tell Steven in the morning and show him Mr. Cleveland's report," Homer replied. "Let's git some rest. See you here for breakfast at 7:00 a.m. sharp."

The next morning after a hearty breakfast prepared by Victoria's mom, the team left for the sheriff's department. When they arrived, Homer handed Steven a copy of the email Zach received from Mr. Cleveland.

"Great! We have a thief and I intend to be the one to read Mr. Smith his Miranda rights! Does Pastor White know?" asked Steven.

"Not yet. Do you want to tell him, or do you want us to tell him, since we're the ones who hired Forensic Auditing Services?" Tom asked.

"You probably should be the ones to tell him but wait until I have Mr. Smith in custody."

"Okay, we're going to talk to Matthew a little more this morning, and then I've got a hankerin' to go fishin' fer awhile to clear my head," Homer said with a big laugh.

A deputy brought Matthew into the interrogation room and within ten minutes, his lawyer pulled up a chair beside him.

"Matthew, we found a gun and silencer in the top drawer of the nightstand in your bedroom. Do you want to tell us about that gun and when you put it there?" asked Tom.

"There is something fishy going on. Someone is trying to frame me. I've never owned a gun and I certainly didn't put one in the nightstand! Let me tell you something

THE ARREST

strange. A uniformed deputy came in my cell the other night with a gun and silencer in an evidence bag. With gloves on, he took the gun out of the bag, handed it to me and asked if it was the gun I used to kill Stephanie.

"I was an idiot to have touched the gun, but it was a natural reaction when the deputy handed it to me. Now you're going to find my prints on the gun. I promise I didn't kill Stephanie!!" a frightened Matthew told Homer. "You've got to believe me. Please find that officer!"

Steven looked at Homer and asked him to step into the hallway with him for a moment. Once out of earshot of Matthew and his attorney, Steven said, "Homer, I know we have deputies that are sometimes unethical, but I find Matthew's story hard to swallow. What do you think?"

"I think he's worried that we are going to hang it all on him," Homer said.

In the meantime, Steven was required to show the Watauga County Magistrate probable cause for the arrest of Rex Smith. Magistrates are a part of the judicial branch of government and are required to exercise independent judgement in the issuance of arrest warrants.

Steven gave Magistrate Cindy Massey a copy of the Forensic Auditing Services Report as evidence for the arrest of Rex Smith. After a thorough review of the evidence presented, the magistrate issued a summons for Mr. Smith's arrest.

While Steven proceeded with arresting Mr. Smith, Homer and Tom drove to the church to meet with Pastor White. When they entered his office, the pastor stood, approached the men, and greeted them.

"Do you have any news to report? How is Matthew?" asked Pastor White.

THE ARREST

"I'm sorry, I just interrupted you before you could even say a word," the pastor said laughing. "How may I help you, Mr. Yancey?"

"Pastor, it's just 'Homer.'"

"Okay, Homer. What's up?"

"We came here today to let ye know that we know who's been stealin' money from the church's offering and alms boxes and to let you know that the cops are gonna pick him up today," Homer said.

Homer read the auditing report to the pastor and then handed him a copy. He expected the pastor to be emotional about one of his members stealing from the church. However, Pastor White nodded his head in agreement, then sat down at his desk. When he regained his composure, he said, "Regretfully, I have to agree with the report, and naturally I am disappointed that one of our members had to resort to stealing.

"We <u>are</u> vulnerable to theft because we expect honesty and trustworthiness. I think I need to discuss future security plans with the deacons.

"Thank you for bringing me the news, gentlemen. I'll plan on visiting Rex tomorrow. I hope the jail will permit it. He may be guilty, but I'm fairly confident he needs a friend right now."

"Do you have any questions?" asked Tom.

"No, but again, thanks for investigating our theft and for your diligence in investigating the murder of Stephanie. Which reminds me, I need to drop by Matthew's house and see how he is holding up."

THE ARREST

"Pastor, ye might want to visit him when you visit Rex," Homer said.

The pastor turned pale, and Tom caught him when he passed out. A few seconds later, he came to. When he realized what had just happened, he was embarrassed. Homer went to get him some water, leaving Tom to attend Pastor White.

As Homer hurried down the hallway looking for a water fountain, he literally ran into a man carrying a mop. The man asked, "Do you need help, sir?"

Homer stopped and told him he needed water to give to the pastor who just passed out. Together they walked to another hallway to the water fountain. The kind man asked if there was anything else Homer needed. Homer scratched his head, a habit he has when thinking to himself.

"I think I might know why I've heard his voice before. I'll just ask him to see if I'm right."

"Did you call me and say that Matthew didn't do it?" He waited for an answer.

"You should take that water to the pastor," the man said.

"Ok, but I'll be right back fer your answer and why ye did that."

After being certain that the pastor was all right, Homer searched the church for the custodian. He was nowhere to be found. Homer decided he'd come back another day and have a little talk with him.

Chapter 11
Fabricated Evidence

Homer sat up in his bed, looked at the clock and saw that it was 3:13 a.m. He reached for his phone and keyed in Tom's number.

"Homer? What? What time is it?" asked Tom as he turned on the lamp beside his bed. "What's up? Are you okay?"

"Tom, how come we didn't pay no attention when Matthew said a deputy came in his cell and got his prints on the gun? Tom, somethang really stinks. I told ye Matthew ain't the killer. The real killer is still out thar and he might be carryin' a badge!"

Tom was certainly awake now and he was following Homer's theory. "Wow, Homer. I think you're on the right track, but we must be cautious at this point and hold these speculations tight to our chests, so to speak. I wouldn't even mention this to the other team members.

"Also, remember, we have law enforcement officers outside our cabin, and they were outside Victoria's room when she was in the hospital. We have to be careful even in the church, especially in the pastor's office. Homer, let's get a sweep of this cabin to make sure we're not being bugged."

"We'll talk later, maybe outside in the fresh air. You're right. We won't take nothing for granted. Night, Tom. Thanks for being my best friend."

"And you're mine, Homer. Good night."

The team met in the kitchen as usual at 7:00 a.m. and were eager to devour the delicious smelling breakfast that Victoria's mother was preparing.

"Yum! What's cooking?" Homer asked as he poured himself a cup of coffee.

"Scrambled eggs, bacon, hashbrowns, and homemade biscuits," interrupted Victoria. "Mom is an excellent cook."

"Your cookin' reminds me of when my mama put vegetables up fer the winter. We used jars, but we called it canning. I find that jarring **is** uncanny," Homer said, which made everyone laugh. "Please excuse me, Mrs. Owen. I need to take Duke fer a walk. I'll be back in a jiffy," Homer announced.

"Homer, may I go with you? asked Tom. "I like walking beside the river and watching the wildlife this time of morning."

"Sure, come on. We'll be back in a minute. Leave us some breakfast," Homer said on his way out the door.

Homer, Tom, and Duke greeted the deputies on the porch, invited them to come inside for breakfast, then walked down the steps.

Once in the yard, Tom said, "That was clever, Homer. Now we should be able to talk."

"What do ye think we should do now?" asked Homer.

"I honestly think we can trust Steven, but he is the chief deputy sheriff and I'm pretty sure his loyalty lies with the department and to the sheriff. Even Steven shouldn't be in our inner circle until he's tested. What do you think?" asked Tom.

"You are probably right about leaving Steven out of what our plans are from here, but he needs to know that Matthew done told us somebody came in his cell in the middle of the night and handed him a gun. We can ask Steven if Matthew's cell is being videotaped. If it is, we can ask to see the tape the night Matthew's talkin' 'bout." Homer commented.

"Good idea, Homer. Let's do it, but after we have some of that good breakfast Mrs. Owen made. I'm hungry," Tom said.

After breakfast, Homer said, "Duke seems to have a little belly problem. I'm gonna take him fer another walk before we go to the jail. Brayden, do you want to walk with us?"

After Homer put the lease on Duke, the two men took him for a walk along the shoreline. After a few minutes of small talk, Homer said, "Brayden I brought ye out here 'cause I think ye can keep a secret and go on a mission fer me."

Brayden was both honored to be trusted and intrigued about what kind of mission Homer was sending him on. "What can I do for you, boss?" Brayden asked.

"Here's the deal. We got reason to think our cabin, our cars and maybe even the pastor's office are bugged. The only ones that know 'bout this are Tom, me, and now you. Nobody else is supposed to know. You got that, Brayden?"

"Yes, sir. Not even the deputies?" Brayden asked.

"Not even them. Now here is what I want ye to do fer me. I want ye to see if ye can find a spy store either in Boone, or some other nearby town. Then I want ye to buy a commercial bug detector. These thangs are designed to vibrate or light up, instead of beeping, so our eavesdroppers won't know we are looking for bugs. This here contraption will help us find where they are at.

"After ye buy it, just leave it in your car. Ye can tell me that you've got it, but I don't want nobody but you and me to know about it, yet. Got it?" Homer instructed.

"Yes, sir."

"Okay, let's go back inside like nothing else happened out here other than we took Duke for his walk," Homer said with a grin.

Once inside, Homer said, "I think we'll let Matthew sweat a little this morning and do some soul searchin'. We're not going to the jail right now. Instead, we're going back to the church. Amelia, I want ye to call the church and see if the pastor will meet us in his office. Brayden, I want ye and Zach to take notes while the pastor is being questioned. Afterwards, we're gonna take a break, then go back to the church and look for more clues in Stephanie's office."

Homer asked, "Amelia, do ye still think the pastor knows more than he told us?"

Amelia had to admit, "Homer, I'm really not sure now, but I guess it would be good to question him," she replied.

"Then think about what should be asked because you'll be the one asking the questions. Me or Tom will bail ye out if we see ye need help," Homer instructed. "Don't be nervous, you'll do real good."

When Homer stepped onto the porch, he stopped to talk to the deputies who had been guarding them since Victoria was shot.

"We'll be gone fer awhile. I gotta tell you that we appreciate the protection you've been givin' us. You've been real nice and act like pros, and we're proud to call y'all friends," Homer said with a big grin.

"Thank you, sir. We'd consider it an honor to be assigned this duty, even if we weren't protecting such a famous detective," one of the men said.

"You guys have a great day. We have to go do some detective work," Tom told the men as he motioned to Homer for them to leave. Homer and Tom shook hands with the deputies, walked down the stairs, and went to Homer's car. The others rode with Zach to the church.

On their way to the church, Tom and Homer discussed the possibility of finding bugs in the cabin and cars. When they arrived at the church, they found Amelia, Brayden, and Tyler in Pastor White's office. Because the pastor was scheduled to meet them in fifteen minutes, Amelia was showing signs of being nervous.

Tom sat beside her on the couch and said, "This is considered to be an investigative interview. I want to give you a few ideas on how to conduct it."

Amelia smiled and said, "That would be great!"

"First, keep an open mind. Just stay focused on the fact that you are asking questions in the hopes that we can learn something new that will help us in this case.

"Ask open-ended questions. That's the kind of question that requires more thought and more than a simple one-word answer. You are trying to encourage him to give a full, meaningful, and deliberate answer.

"Just start with easy questions, like how long he's been the pastor here. Did he know Stephanie before hiring her? How long had he known her?

"As he provides answers to your questions throughout the interview, keep your opinions to yourself. Let him do the talking. Focus on the facts as he gives them. Tell him we have interviewed other members of his church. You might mention their names and get his reaction or comments. Also, ask if he thinks they are trustworthy. How long has he known them? Finally, give him the assurance that his answers will be held confidential and that we appreciate all he is doing to help with this investigation. You will do great, Amelia. We think this training will be a valuable lesson for you. If you get stuck and need us, just look over at us and we will take over."

Homer smiled, "Are you ready, Amelia?"

"Yes, sir!" she answered.

The pastor opened the door to his office. The team members smiled as they stood. Homer broke the ice when he said, "Please come into Pastor White's office, sir." Everyone chuckled.

Homer extended his hand to the pastor and asked if he knew everyone. "Yes, everyone but this young lady," he said pointing to Amelia.

"This here's Amelia Davis. She's a lawyer and the newest member of our team. She's got a few questions fer ye," Homer said as he signaled for her to begin.

The questioning lasted for about forty-five minutes. When Amelia thanked the pastor for coming in to help clarify a few facts pertinent to the case, the team stood and shook Pastor White's hand. After a short time of small talk, the team excused themselves, leaving the pastor to lock up the church.

Once in the car, the first thing Amelia said was, "Whew! I'm glad that's over. I think I'll stick to being an attorney for the team instead of an investigator!"

"Don't sell yourself short, Amelia. You did great. I'm proud of you," her brother Brayden said.

"After the pastor's gone fer a while, we can go back inside and see if we can find more clues in Stephanie's office," Homer said. "Right now, let's go grab somethang to drink from that thar gas station we went by on our way here. Then we can go to Wilbur Lake, find us a picnic table whar it's nice and peaceful."

"That sounds really nice. When do we get to play on the river again, Homer?" asked Zach.

"We gotta do some more lookin' around in Mrs. Stephanie's office, then go see Matthew. Sorry, Zach, we ain't gonna have that fun day 'til this weekend," Homer replied.

"That's okay. The weekend is only two days away," Zach responded.

Brayden found a vacant table beside the lake and handed out the cold drinks. As they relaxed, they noticed the presence of wildflowers along the river's shoreline.

Brayden asked, "What exactly is a WILDflower?

FABRICATED EVIDENCE

Tom said, "I can answer that, Brayden. I have a friend who is a Master Gardner, and she said a wildflower is a flower that grows without any help from people. They grow naturally in their environment. People can grow wildflowers in their garden, but most wildflowers are native plants and grow in woods, meadows, wetlands – anywhere they adapted to grow."

Brayden responded, "My college science professor must have loved wildflowers because she brought some to class nearly every day. She told us that wildflowers improve the quality of air and water. Another thing she told us was that the roots of wildflowers help to stabilize the soil and hold on to nutrients that might otherwise be washed away in the rain. Their presence can improve soil health, prevent erosion, and improve air and water quality.

"I thought my professor was a little kooky at first until I let her comments sink in. Now I appreciate wildflowers," Brayden added.

As they relaxed, they noticed a large boat on the river. Written on the side of the boat were the words, "Appalachian State University Dive Team."

Brayden asked, "Why would the University have a dive team?"

"When Homer was about to speak to the Criminal Justice class at Appalachian, I overheard a student say he was signed up to take the new Search and Rescue class so he would be qualified to be on a law enforcement dive team when he graduates. I guess those young people are part of that class and they are out here practicing," responded Tom.

"Maybe we should take a course like that," Brayden said with excitement.

Several students clad in scuba gear slipped into the cold water. Those aboard the boat were apparently monitoring the divers' locations and depth. After a few minutes, one of the divers resurfaced holding what appeared to be a large plastic bag tied with a rope. The divers climbed back into the boat. The team watched intently as someone onboard opened the bag and pulled out what looked like a shovel.

Homer had been following everything that was happening and when he saw the shovel, he looked at Tom with excitement in his eyes. "Tom! Could fingerprints still be on a shovel that was in a plastic bag in the river water?"

"Probably not. For one thing, sweat glands secrete primarily water. Therefore, finger or palm prints are usually dissolved in water. The second thing is those students are passing around the shovel which is compromising any fingerprints originally on the shovel, anyway," Tom explained.

"Dadgum! Well, we don't have no proof that those kids who accidentally found a shovel are holding the one that the killer used," Homer said.

"However, we could ask the professor for the shovel and explain that we are fairly confident that it's evidence in a murder case," Tom suggested.

"Tyler, go to the University tomorrow and see if ye can find the professor of that class. Show him your credentials and ask him if you can have the shovel," Homer instructed. "Don't tell him that there might not be no prints on it. If he thinks the same thang, just tell him that all we gotta do is show the shovel to the jury and tell 'em it was pulled out of the river close to the grave.

"Okay, break's over. Let's git outta here and git back at lookin' around Stephanie's office before we go to the jail. The pastor more than likely done left fer the day.

"Pastor White's gotta lot to keep him on his knees lately. First, Stephanie was killed, then he finds out somebody's stealin' from the offering box and some of the members of his church had to come here fer questioning. Matthew is put in investigative detention and might be under arrest if 'em prints on the gun and silencer match his.

Oh yeah, then Rex Smith is arrested. Pastor White has a pretty heavy burden right now and he might be thinkin' he'd better git right with the Lord. So, next time ye see him, give him a break. Ye might even ask if ye can pray for him." Homer said.

Two days later the final forensic report was emailed to Zach. The bullet which was found in Stephanie's grave was sent to the forensic pathologists who were assigned the task of identifying the fingerprints found on the gun and silencer. It was not a surprise to Homer that Matthew's prints were a perfect match. Steven called to discuss the report with Homer.

"I really hate to hear what's in this report 'cause he's my cousin. But I think ye need to go in front of the magistrate, present the forensic report as evidence and ask fer a warrant to arrest Matthew Wright fer the murder of Stephanie."

Within thirty minutes of hearing the details of the forensic report, the magistrate signed the arrest warrant for Matthew Wright. Deputy Adamson went to the holding area, Cell Four.

"Mr. Wright, I have a warrant for your arrest, turn around and put your hands behind your back," Deputy Steven Adamson insisted. Matthew did not resist. After Matthew was handcuffed, Steven said, "You are being arrested for the murder of Stephanie Lynn Wright." He was then read the Miranda rights.

Matthew was very nervous as he and Steven walked towards the booking area. Thoughts flooded his mind about all the bad things he had heard about being incarcerated. He thought of his friend, Charlie, who was arrested for drunk driving. Charlie had shared with Matthew the entire humiliating booking process including the full-body search.

Due to the high-profile coverage of Stephanie's death, the Yancey Investigative Services' handling of the case, and the seriousness of the charges against him, the decision was made to house Matthew in a single jail cell. For this decision, Matthew was grateful.

Once he was placed in the cell, Steven removed the handcuffs. Matthew sat on his bed, leaned forward with his head in his hands, and wept.

Chapter 12
Get Rid of the Bugs!

"Homer, the falcon has landed," Brayden said with a wide grin.

"I ain't never seen no bird like that before," Homer said with a wink.

"Really? Then let's go outside and I'll show it to you." Brayden said.

"I'm rite behind ya," responded Homer.

The men went outside for a few minutes and when they were sure that no one was watching, Brayden lifted the rear hatch to his SUV.

"I think the bug detector I bought is just what you were wanting. What do you think?"

"It's just what I wanted. **Keep that thang in the car** 'til I tell ye to bring it in," Homer instructed.

Once inside, Homer told everyone to skedaddle and enjoy the sunshine. He looked at Brayden and asked, "Stay'n or go'n?"

"I plan to stay here because I have some work to do. I'll see you guys later," he said as everyone else quickly cleared the room.

"First, I plan to git the fish wrappers, if I can find 'em," Homer said as he started walking around looking for something.

"What in the world is a fish wrapper?" Brayden asked.

GET RID OF THE BUGS

"That's what my paw used to call the newspaper. Have you seen 'em? They come here ever week — the *High-Country Press* and the *Mountain Times*.

"I think Mrs. Owens was reading them during breakfast," Brayden said as he walked to the kitchen. "I found them, Homer."

Brayden handed the newspapers to Homer who was standing in the living room.

"Great goobly woobly! The headline for the *High-Country Press* says, "Boone H.S. Principal Accused of Killing Wife." The *Mountain Times* headline is, "Boone H.S. Principal Arrested for Murder."

Homer read the High-Country Press article aloud. "Boone High School Principal, Matthew Wright, was arrested today and charged with the murder of his wife,

Stephanie Lynn Wright. Mrs. Wright was the secretary for Hickory Grove Baptist Church and was reported missing a few mon_{ths ago}..." Homer stopped reading and just looked up at Brayden. There was an expression of deep sadness on Homer's face.

Just then, Brayden heard a deputy's radio sound.

Both deputies came inside Homer's cabin and informed him that they would have to leave for a while.

"I hope everythangs ok. Be careful guys, and don't worry 'bout us, we'll be fine," Homer responded.

After they left, Homer told Brayden, "I'm glad we got some time to check for bugs, so let's git to work. First, let's take Duke fer a walk."

GET RID OF THE BUGS

While walking beside the river, Homer said, "Brayden, I think it might be good fer us to go to McDonald's. Nobody can hear us talkin' and ye can put that thang together in your car. If ye need more room, we'll go inside and git us a table in the corner. I'll git us a coke and a snack. What ye think?"

"That's a great idea, Homer," Brayden responded.

They decided it would be better to assemble the bug detector inside McDonald's. It took about twenty minutes for Brayden to assemble the unit while Homer read the instructions aloud.

Tom walked into McDonald's to grab a cup of coffee and was surprised to see Homer and Brayden sitting at a booth apparently trying to assemble something.

"Hey, Buddy."

Homer told him they just finished putting the detector together and were going to go back to the cabin and start the sweep.

"Homer, I've been thinking back on a class I taught on what to do if you suspect someone has placed a listening device in your home. I reminded the class that if the source of a bug is likely to be a law enforcement agency, then it may be illegal to tamper with it. If that is what you suspect, Homer, then our simply being aware of its presence must suffice.

"But I will say that any steps you take towards uncovering a listening device should start with this — if they are truly determined to hear us, we will probably never know, but that shouldn't stop us from trying to find out. So, I say we should sweep the cabin and if we locate any bugs, we need to mark the location with colored tape and be diligent not to divulge any sensitive information," Tom advised.

"Ok, let's git with it," Homer said, then flashed that famous grin.

The three men drove back to the cabin. They decided that when they needed to communicate, they would cuff their hand and whisper into each other's ear.

Brayden whispered to Homer, "Let's start in the living room." Homer did a thumbs up. After locating two devices, they moved to the dining room and then to every room of the cabin, meticulously searching lighting fixtures, sockets, cable boxes, communication ports, Wi-Fi routers, and all available cell phones. Twelve listening devices were located, marked, and left undisturbed.

Tom whispered, "When the team members return, everyone's cell phone and laptop or tablet should be swept." Again, Homer gave a thumbs up.

The team members finally came in about two hours later. Their first comments pertained to the whereabouts of the deputies since they were not outside the door guarding the cabin. Homer told them they said they needed to leave for a while.

"Since they are county deputies, I didn't ask for an explanation," Homer said. His answer satisfied the team. Homer added, "Let's go down to the river. I've got somethang important to tell you."

Even though there were surprised expressions on faces, no one argued.

GET RID OF THE BUGS

When everyone assembled at the river, Homer said, "We know this cabin, maybe our phones, laptops and tablets are bugged. I want y'all to whisper in someone's ear if ye need to share sensitive stuff. After supper we can use the bug detector we got and search your personal stuff. We'll do one at a time after we eat. Y'all keep talkin' 'bout how much fun ye done had on the river. Got it? When we are in the cabin, write your questions or comments down and give them to me."

After an hour, Homer felt that all devices found in the cabin were labeled and their location written in his notebook. In addition to the bugs found in the cabin, bugs were also found in the team's cell phones, personal laptops, and tablets.

Homer wrote a note and held it up for everyone to see. He thanked everyone for their cooperation and told them, especially Zach and Victoria and her parents, to avoid discussing any of this once in their rooms. He also suggested no phone calls tonight. "Got it?" he asked.

Everyone decided to call it a night and walked down the hallway to their rooms. Homer stopped Victoria's parents, grinned, and started writing. In the note, he said, "Thank ye fer being here with us. I'm sorry ye gotta go by the same rules I done gave the team, but it's important we don't mess up this case. I hope you understand and are willing to work through this with us." They both nodded affirmatively and did a thumbs up.

"Good night, Homer," Mrs. Owen said as she kissed Homer on the cheek. "You are a wonderful role model for your team. Have a good night. Any requests for breakfast?"

"Waffles would be good," Homer replied.

GET RID OF THE BUGS

"Waffles it is. See you at 7:00 a.m."

Mr. Owen said, "Good night, Homer. Don't let the bedbugs bite."

"I ain't heard that saying in a 'coon's age," Homer laughed aloud. "Night, Mr. Owen. Ye had better git here early fer breakfast 'cause if ye don't, 'em waffles might be long gone," Homer said grinning.

After walking Duke, Homer locked the cabin, turned out the lights, except for the lamp in the living room, then he and Duke went to their room. Duke jumped onto the bed and was asleep in less than three minutes. Homer, on the other hand, stayed awake for quite a while thinking about finding the listening devices and wondering not only who installed them, but why and when they were set up and connected. Because he suspected it was law enforcement listening in, Homer wondered if he could trust Steven with this information. After tossing and turning for a couple of hours, Homer finally went to sleep.

After having lost sleep the night before, Homer was late for breakfast. Everyone wanted him to get some rest, but they decided to play a joke on him. When Homer came into the kitchen, all the waffles appeared to have been eaten. One by one, the team members thanked Mrs. Owen for the delicious breakfast and poured more coffee and sat down.

Homer just stood looking at the empty waffle iron with a pitiful expression. Everyone roared with laughter and Mrs. Owen opened the oven, pulled out a full plate of waffles, and handed them to Homer.

"Real funny, guys. Thanks, Mrs. O," Homer said and devoured his breakfast.

GET RID OF THE BUGS

"Homer, Steven wants you to call him," Tom said. Homer reached for his cell phone and called Steven. "Mornin,' Steven, what's up?" asked Homer.

"I think something is strange here at the office. One of our deputies who had violations against him is being promoted this morning. I thought you might want to come down for the ceremony at 9:00 a.m. and listen to the sheriff tell why this deputy was singled out for a promotion."

There was a small gathering at the promotion ceremony for Deputy **Bill Carpenter**, held in the sheriff's conference room.

"Deputy **Carpenter**, please stand next to me," the sheriff instructed.

Deputy **Carpenter** walked to the front where his commanding officer stood.

"First, allow me to thank everyone for being here this morning. We take the promotions of our deputies seriously because they don't come easy. Deputy **Carpenter** has had a few bumps in the road on his journey to arrive at this point.

"On the state level, **Carpenter** has been exonerated from his two violations. The first was a trapping and hunting violation pertaining to wild-life tagging. The second violation was regarding a false allegation, which was a violation of the state's new TRUST Act.

"Deputy **Carpenter** scored high marks on the required test for this promotion. In June, **Bill** will be a four-year veteran with the sheriff's office where he has worked as a patrol deputy and as a drone pilot for the sheriff's office. He currently is serving in the department's criminal division detention facility."

The Sheriff turned to **Deputy Carpenter** and said, "**Bill** has been married only a little over a year and his bride is with us today. **Peggy**, come up here and stand with **Bill**, please."

"**Bill**, I have heard nothing but good things about you from your former supervisors and your colleagues at the Watauga County Sheriff's Department," said Sheriff Reed. "And I am proud to promote you to sergeant today because of your hard work and dedication. Keep up the good work."

Those in the room applauded as the **sheriff handed** Deputy **Carpenter the sergeant badge. Bill** shook hands with the sheriff and then turned to his wife, Peggy, and gave her a kiss.

Steven turned to Homer with a look of disgust. "Let's go get a cup of coffee down the street," Steven suggested.

Homer caught Tom's attention then tilted his head and shrugged his shoulders. Tom gave a thumbs up.

After ordering coffee, the men found a table in the back. Immediately, Steven said, "Something is odd about that promotion. It doesn't bother me that someone is being brought up in the ranks, but I've watched this guy and he seems to me to want to do things on his terms. He isn't a team player and is possibly unethical. Oh! Did I just describe Sergeant Carpenter or Sheriff Reed? So, there you have it," he said with a smile. "I just needed to walk away for a few minutes. Thanks for coming with me. What's up with you guys this morning?"

GET RID OF THE BUGS

"We got four thangs. One, we want to know how to go 'bout finding the deputy who went into Matthew's cell and got his fingerprints on the gun and silencer. Two, our cabin's been bugged and we've found lots of 'em. We think it's sheriff's office bugs. Three, Tom and I wondered if we could trust ye with this sensitive stuff and ye just proved we can. Four, when this investigation is done, would ye think 'bout coming on-board with Yancey Investigative Services? I'll give ye a salary of $100,000 and a new car. Since you ain't married, ye gotta move to Oneonta. We'll give ye a place to stay fer free in the Yancey bunk house."

Tom interrupted, "It isn't the kind of bunk house you may be envisioning; it's a mansion. Homer is worth over $5.2 million dollars, and he treats us royally."

Homer asked, "How 'bout it, Steven?"

"Well, let me think about it," Steven replied. Less than 10 seconds later, Steven said, "I'm all in. Thanks, Homer. That's a terrific benefits package. If you knew what my current salary is, you would laugh. I eagerly accept your offer, Homer. I like working with you guys and already feel like I am part of the team," Steven said as he shook hands with Homer and Tom. "Our current priority is to find Stephanie's murderer."

"Homer, you were wondering how we go should about establishing who went into Matthew's cell and got his fingerprints on the gun and silencer. As a detective, I hate to admit that getting someone's fingerprints is easier than you might think.

"First, I think you need to start with asking Matthew what day it was that a deputy came into his cell. Second, you can find out from Matthew the approximate time the deputy came in. Third, ask him if he happened to see the deputy's name badge on his uniform.

"I think these are good starting points. Then find out what shift it was and if anyone saw the deputy. Was he carrying anything? Did he stay in the office long? Is there anything the other deputies remember about that timeframe?"

"That is great strategy," Tom said. "but why do you keep saying 'you' can this or that instead of 'we'? I guess I was assuming that you would be in on the investigation."

"I can guide you in the process, but if I openly get involved, the internal affairs guys will take over the investigation. It's not that I don't trust or believe that they will do a good job, it's just that I think Yancey Investigative Services should get some answers first. Since you are the lead detectives it would only be appropriate. Then you can turn your findings over to internal affairs."

"So, tell us somethang 'bout Internal Affairs, so we'll know what's gonna happen next. What are they gonna do?" asked Homer.

Chapter 13
Blue Wall of Silence

"Internal affairs (often known as IA) is a division of a law enforcement agency that investigates incidents and allegations of lawbreaking and professional misconduct attributed to officers on the force. It is therefore a mechanism of limited self-governance, 'a police force policing itself'," Steven explained.

"Internal affairs investigators must persistently work at uncovering the facts. The decisions they make during the investigation have power. They decide the course of the investigation and what questions are going to be asked. I personally think police and sheriff departments need investigators who will relentlessly pursue the facts while conducting an objective investigation. The best investigators, in my opinion, keep asking questions in order to get the truth for the best conclusion possible.

So, as you can see, I do think that they will do a good job, but I also think Yancey Investigative Service will, too. You need to have first shot at it.

"One more thing, it is only internal affairs that can determine whether a deputy has committed a crime. The results can be prosecution and prison time. So, as you can see, at some point, you will have to turn over the results of our investigation to them," Steven explained.

"So, you're telling me we won't have to worry 'bout proving our case to the sheriff that one of his deputies is guilty, we just need to git 'em folks in internal affairs workin' on it. Does the sheriff have to call 'em?" asked Homer.

"In Watauga County, the chief deputy is responsible for overseeing the internal affairs function of the sheriff's office," Steven said with a grin. "Therefore, when you finish your investigation, you can hand your report to me.

"Now as far as the listening devices in your cabin and personal property, I recommend that you don't touch them. Let's deal with one issue at a time. Do you think you guys can whisper for a few days?" Steven asked with a grin.

"I think we can handle that," Homer replied. "Do ye want to meet here fer coffee ever day?"

"What if we meet as needed. If you need to talk, just text me. Your phone conversations are bugged, but not your text messages. That's the way I will also be in touch with you. Does this sound good to you?" he asked.

"Sounds good, and by the way, you're gonna to be a real help to our team," commented Homer.

"Are you sure texting is safe?" asked Tom.

"The sheriff's office has to obtain a subpoena to read your opened and unopened messages. But they have to let you know once they have requested this access from your provider. Have you been notified?"

"Nope," responded Homer.

"Then our texting will be fine," Steven reassured them.

"When can we start askin' 'bout who on earth went into Matthew's cell and got his fingerprints?" asked Homer.

"We need to meet with Matthew first. How does this afternoon sound? We can meet in the interrogation room at 2:00 p.m. I will allow Matthew to call his attorney so he can be present for our questioning. We will proceed from there," replied Steven. "By the way," he said with a grin. "How about bringing a picture of that bunkhouse with you when you come?" he asked Homer.

"I can do that for ye," Homer said.

"See you at 2:00 p.m., boss," Steven said, then shook Homer's hand. He nodded at Tom and smiled.

"You don't have to wait that long, Steven. I have a picture of the bunkhouse on my phone. I can text it to you right now," Tom said.

"Okay, sounds good," he said as he waited for Tom's text.

"You have to be kidding me! That's no bunkhouse!" Steven said while flashing a big smile.

"It's like I said, 'I'm all in!'" laughed Steven.

"Let's git a move on and find out who murdered Stephanie! See ye at 2:00 p.m.," Homer said. He and Tom left.

Matthew was brought into the interrogation room and his attorney was already waiting for him. "What's this all about?" Matthew asked. His attorney shrugged his shoulders indicating that he didn't know.

At 2:00 p.m., Homer, Tom, and Chief Deputy Adamson entered the room and sat across from Matthew and his attorney.

"Matthew, we've got some questions fer ye," Homer said, opening the dialogue. "Matthew, let me say I'm sorry we didn't look into what you done said 'bout the deputy who done come in your cell and somehow got your prints on the gun and silencer. This here's why we're meetin' with ye today, and why your attorney's here," commented Homer.

"Your answers will determine if there is a need to further investigate this matter. If a deputy can be identified and is suspected of this kind of action, as Chief Deputy Sheriff, I have the authority to ask internal affairs to review our findings and to further investigate. If the deputy is found guilty, he can be dismissed, demoted, or arrested.

Therefore, Mr. Wright, I wish to advise you that you are being questioned as part of an official investigation of the sheriff's office. Do you understand, sir?" asked Steven.

"Yes, I understand. I am grateful that you men will investigate and I promise to tell you the truth," Matthew said, then added, "I'd shake your hand, but these cuffs prevent me."

"Matthew, only give us an answer to the question we ask. What day did the deputy come into your cell?" asked Tom who was writing Matthew's answers down.

"It was the day before you went to search my house," Matthew replied.

"Can you give us an approximate time the deputy came into your cell?" asked Steven.

"I can give you the exact time. When the light in my cell came on, it startled me, so I asked him what time it was. He told me it was two o'clock in the morning." Matthew replied.

"I reckon I got one more question. Did you look at the name on the deputy's badge?" asked Homer.

"No, I didn't think to read his name badge," Matthew responded.

"Can you give us a description of the deputy?" asked Tom.

"Not really, I was very sleepy, and when he handed me that gun, I wasn't concerned about his appearance. I was upset he said it was the gun that killed Stephanie. I'm sorry, Homer," Matthew said as he hung his head.

"That's okay, Matthew, we'll find him. We appreciate your cooperation, and we reserve the right to recall you for further questioning should we deem it necessary," Steven said, then motioned for a deputy to take Matthew back to his cell.

"Ready fer a cuppa Joe, Steven?" Homer asked.

"Sure, I could use a good cup of coffee. I'll meet you there," he responded.

Once at the coffee shop, Homer approached the counter and placed the order.

"Three coffees fer three detectives," Homer said as he set the drinks on the table. "I reckon it went okay with Matthew. I'm fixin' to go hunt fer the guy that busted into Matthew's cell and I reckon it's gonna take talking to a bunch of deputies. We ain't gonna take our own sweet time on this. We gotta talk to the ones who was on duty the night Matthew's talking 'bout," Homer said.

"You are absolutely right. I am going to have to let you guys investigate from here and then turn your findings over to me. If you can confirm who you think it is, then you can turn your report over to me and I can ask for an investigation from internal affairs," Steven instructed.

"I'm gittin' mad as a box of frogs. We've gotta find this guy and git a confession from him. He did a dumb thing going into Matthew's cell like he did, which tells me that he ain't the 'big dog,' he's jest the one wearing the collar and being pulled ever which way. We've gotta figger out who's yankin' his chain and why," Homer commented.

"So, this is why they say you are such a famous detective. Good thinking, Homer. I agree with you," said Steven.

Tom patted Homer on the back and grinned.

Meanwhile, the team had been hard at work all day. They were anxious to make their reports, but knew at this point they would have to use note paper to communicate since listening devices were in the cabin.

When Homer and Tom arrived at the cabin, Homer asked if the deputies would like to join the team for dinner.

One of the deputies asked if they could instead join them for breakfast. "Sir, we are pretty tired tonight."

"Absolutely. Are ye up to standing guard duty tonight?" Homer asked.

"We've decided to work tonight in shifts. We'll take turns resting. I think we'll be good to go in the morning, sir," one of the deputies said with a wide opened yawn. "Sorry, sir," he said with a laugh.

"I'll see you later when I take Duke fer his evenin' constitution. Y'all come in when you want some coffee," Homer added.

Once inside, the table was set, and the meal was being served. It appeared that Brayden had already handed out note pads and pens and everyone was eager to hear about Homer and Tom's day and to report on theirs.

"Mrs. Owen, I've been meanin' to put some meat on these bones and your cookin' sure has done it fer me. As a thank ye, we'll be goin' to the Dan'l Boone Restaurant tomorrow night, my treat. Victoria, are you up to eatin' out with that guy you married? You'll have seven chaperones," Homer said.

"I think that would be wonderful," she said as she leaned in to give Homer a kiss on the cheek.

After dinner, Homer picked up his note pad and nodded to Brayden to give his report. Brayden took the cue.

Brayden had already started writing about going to Appalachian State University and meeting with the Criminal Justice professor who took his Search and Rescue class out on a boat on the Watauga River. Brayden held up a shovel and again wrote on his note pad that the professor gave him the shovel to use as evidence in Mrs. Wright's murder investigation.

No noise was heard as they all put their hands together mimicking applause.

It was Homer and Tom's turn to report on what they had been doing today. Tom wrote that he and Homer went to a promotion ceremony at the sheriff's department. They had a lengthy meeting with Chief Deputy Adamson regarding finding listening devices in the cabin. During their meeting, Homer made an offer to hire Deputy Adamson at the conclusion of the investigation of Stephanie's murder. He accepted Homer's offer and plans to relocate to Alabama and live in the bunkhouse. We also met with Matthew and his attorney. We asked Matthew several questions for clarification in an effort to identify the deputy who entered Matthew's cell and got his fingerprints on the gun and silencer.

The graveyard shift, as it is sometimes called, is from 11:00 p.m. to 7:00 a.m. at the sheriff's office. In order to interview deputies on this shift, Homer and Tom left the cabin at 1:00 a.m. and drove to the Watauga County Sheriff's Department. They signed in at the front desk and informed the deputy-in-charge that Chief Deputy Adamson had given them permission to interview the deputies working on this shift. The sergeant behind the desk said he had already received confirmation that Homer and Tom would be allowed to interview the on-duty deputies. They were given visitor badges and were allowed entry.

Steven met Homer and Tom when they entered. Then he led them into the room where the deputies were waiting. He told Homer and Tom that he wanted to introduce them and explain why they were there.

"Men, I would like to introduce to you Homer Yancey and Tom Lynch with Yancey Investigative Services. They are investigating the murder of Stephanie Wright. These men are here tonight to ask you a few questions because there is reason to believe we have within our ranks a deputy that may be guilty of misconduct by the intentional fabrication of evidence.

BLUE WALL OF SILENCE

"I wish to advise you that you are being questioned as part of an official investigation that has the potential of being given to internal affairs for additional review. You are entitled to all the rights and privileges guaranteed by the laws and the Constitution of North Carolina and the Constitution of the United States, including the right not to be compelled to incriminate yourself.

"I further wish to advise you that if you refuse to answer Mr. Yancey's or Mr. Lynch's questions, you will be in violation of Sheriff's Office General Order 420 Code of Conduct, Section VII Subsection 2. If you do answer, neither your statements nor evidence which is gained by reason of such statements, can be used against you in any criminal proceeding. However, these statements may be used against you in relation to violation of Sheriff's Office General Orders. Before I turn the questioning over to the Yancey team, are there any questions?" asked Steven.

No one asked a question, so Steven nodded to Homer to begin the questioning. Steven left the room.

Tom said that he and Homer were aware that the deputies were about to be questioned while still in their work environment. He assured everyone that they intended to honor the fact that the deputies have a lot to do in a county the size of Watauga, so he and Homer would question them individually, with the option of returning, if necessary. Tom said that Deputy Adamson provided them with a list of deputies, and they intended to ask only a few questions.

Tom motioned for Homer to come over to where he was standing. "Homer, I just wanted to remind you of

'The blue wall of silence,' in case you want to address it."

"I ain't gonna beat 'round the bush. We've gotta ask ye some tough questions and want ye to be honest. We've got an inklin' that a serious crime was done here and we need answers. We know all 'bout that thar 'blue wall of silence,' and I git it. I'd be happier than a dead pig in the sunshine if you'd drop that rite now 'cause this here's an official investigation. If we ask ye a question 'bout another officer and ye know the rite answer but you choose to do that blue wall thang, then you'll be barkin' up the wrong tree with me 'cause you'll be in a heap 'o trouble. It's called perjury. Do I make myself clear?" Homer asked.

To ensure that each deputy was questioned in private, Tom and Homer used the interrogation room.

Fourteen deputies were questioned, which took nearly two hours.

When all the deputies had been questioned, Tom thanked them for their cooperation. He informed them that Yancey Investigative Services reserved the right to recall a deputy for further questioning if needed.

As Homer and Tom were leaving the building, Steven caught up with them and asked, "May I buy you a hot cuppa Joe?"

Chapter 14
Men in Black

"I think I'll just have a nice cold H_2O," said Homer.

After Tom returned with coffee and water, he had hardly sat down when Steven asked, "Did you learn anything from the interviews?"

"We talked to fourteen deputies and three actually told us the truth 'bout what done happened that thar morning. All three pointed the finger at Bill Carpenter as the one who woke Matthew up when he went into his cell. There ain't no proof 'cause they said the video camera in Matthew's cell was turned off.

"According to all three deputies, Bill walked into the open deputy work area and said, 'Hey, I just noticed that the video camera in Matthew Wright's holding cell wasn't turned on, so I turned it back on.' He then told us, 'Let's get sharp, guys! We were told to observe him. I noticed it and turned it back on. I'm going home. Let the sheriff know if Mr. Wright does anything unusual.' He told everyone goodnight, then walked to the rear of the building and exited.

"But here's the good part. While one of the deputies was in the restroom, he looked out the window right after Bill left the building. The deputy said he saw Bill walk up to a guy in uniform who appeared to have been waitin' on him because as soon as he saw Bill, they started talking. the deputy was confident it was Bill because of his tall, slender frame. However, he didn't recognize the other man. Bill pulled somethang out of his pocket and gave it to the guy. They talked briefly before they left. Do ye think Bill might have handed off the gun and silencer with Matthew's prints on them?" asked Homer.

"That's a really good question and we have got to find out. Right now, it looks suspicious, however, I would only be speculating," replied Steven.

"We're gonna head on back to the cabin and tell all this to Zach so he can git ye a report to give to internal affairs," Homer said.

"Good work, detectives. It is commendable that you got three deputies to trust you enough to tell you the truth." Steven said.

"Thanks, Steven, but I think we were more nervous than the deputies we interviewed," Tom said laughing.

"We have got to figure out who the man is and what was handed to him by Bill," Tom said. "Any ideas, Steven?"

"None whatsoever, but the information the deputies gave you this morning will be in the report to internal affairs. The improper behavior and lack of honesty displayed by some members of our profession over the last few years has raised questions and concern with the public. There are merited occasions when a law enforcement officer's lack of integrity and unethical acts are so egregious, they cannot go unpunished. I believe this situation is one of those occasions," Steven said as he sipped his coffee.

"We ain't had much sleep and are gittin' plum tuckered out, so we need to git on back to the cabin and git Zach working on this fer ye. I assume ye will try to get a few hours of shuteye before ye go back to work. I know we will, so when do ye want us to bring ye the report? I don't want to hand it to anybody 'cept ye," Homer said.

"Let's just meet here around 11:00 a.m.," Steven replied.

"Sounds good. See you then. Stay safe, Steven," Tom said.

"Yeah, you guys stay safe, too. We are dealing with a cold-blooded murderer, and he could possibly be the same person who shot Victoria. Watch your back at all times," Steven said as he left.

Homer and Tom said hello to the two deputies standing by their door, then they went inside. Since it was still early, the men entered the cabin as quietly as possible.

"Thanks for all your great questions today, Tom. Anythang ye got on your chest we need to talk 'bout before headin' to bed?" asked Homer.

"Not right now. I'm too tired to think. Go to bed, Homer, we'll talk later," Tom replied.

"I need to take Duke for a walk, then I'll get gittin' some shuteye myself. Night Tom. Let's go Duke," Homer said.

Duke was doing circles. "Ok, boy, let's go," Homer said as he stepped out the door.

The two deputies were not on the porch, so Homer pulled on Duke and quickly went back inside.

"Somethangs going on. The two deputies ain't on the porch, and it's kinda quiet out thar." Homer called

Brayden's phone. It was 4:00 a.m. and everyone was in bed.

"Brayden, wake up everyone and get them in the living room quickly." When they all arrived, Homer told everyone to stay away from the windows.

"Zach, go get Victoria and her parents and bring 'em to the living room with us."

"Yes, sir," Zach replied and hastily went down the hall to his room.

When Zach, Victoria, and her parents walked into the living room, they saw two men in dark business suits standing facing Homer.

"Mr. Yancey, we didn't mean to startle you, but we are from the FBI," one agent said. He motioned for the

Agent Ron Rutledge, and this is Agent Jeff Todd. For about a month, we have been surveilling the two deputies who were assigned to protect you because we were given a tip that these men were not legitimate, and we are instructed to keep you safe."

"Unfortunately, Mr. Yancey, neither of the men are Watauga County deputies. After taking them into custody, we learned they were hired to spy on you to learn the development of your investigation. We know your cabin is bugged and we allowed it because we were watching those who were watching you," Agent Todd said. "I believe we can remove the listening devices now, if that's ok."

"Tyler stood and said, "We are grateful for your protection. Do you have any idea who hired these two men?""We have our suspicions, but are still investigating," replied Agent Rutledge.

MEN IN BLACK

"Well, Mr. Yancey, we will be removing those listening devices if now is a good time for you. Young man, you want to help us?" the agent asked Tyler.

Tyler smiled at Homer who gave him a smile and a thumbs up.

"What's your name young man?" asked Agent Rutledge as they took the first bug from the lamp.

"Watch it fella, he's one of my stars. So back off, you can't have him!" Homer said, which made everyone laugh.

"Sir, we are going to charge these two men with impersonating an officer. Citizens have to put a lot of trust in law enforcement. Police officers and county deputies are employed to ensure that citizens follow the laws of the state, and as such, exercise a great deal of power over everyday people.

"Unfortunately, sometimes criminals attempt to take advantage of this power and abuse it. Impersonating a law enforcement officer is illegal in all fifty states, but like these two men, impersonation still happens.

"In most states, including North Carolina, the act of impersonating a law enforcement officer is considered a misdemeanor. However, there could be some serious consequences that these men might face if charged.

"According to the statute and codes in North Carolina, if convicted, they could spend up to two years behind bars. That's quite a lengthy amount of time. And they could face a penalty as high as $2,000.

"Mr. Yancey, these men will be turned over to the Boone Police Department. Another thing, Mr. Yancey, you are doing all the right things. We're not taking over your investigation. We were just told to watch these two imposters, which we did. They will be booked and processed at the jail. Any questions?"

"Yes, can Chief Deputy Adamson be trusted?" asked Homer.

"Completely, sir."

When the agents left, Homer said, "Ok, all together now, 'exhale.'" That made everyone laugh.

Mrs. Owen, I know I offered to take everyone to dinner tonight, but would you mind if we go tomorrow night? I think we are all going to be too tired tonight to go out. So, if you have any leftovers from a meal, would you mind feeding us tonight and setting a place for one more?" asked Homer.

"I am here to help, Homer. It would be my pleasure," Mrs. Owens replied.

I'm gonna ask Steven to eat with us so everyone can meet him. Who wants to go with us to the coffee shop?" asked Homer.

Zach and Victoria raised their hands at the same time.

"So, young lady, are you permitted out in the real world?" asked Tom.

Victoria's mother interrupted. "She is doing great and I think it would be good for her to tag along. What do you think, Zach?"

"Yeah, she'll be fine, because she can lean on me if she needs to, don't you agree, sweetie?" Zach asked.

Victoria leaned over and gave Zach a long, sweet kiss.

"Turn away, Mr. and Mrs. Owen," laughed Tyler.

"Come on, Duke, let's take a walk," Homer said. Duke eagerly ran to the door. After Homer put the leash on Duke, he said, "Looks like his eyeballs are floating! Let's try this again, Duke," and they went outside.

When Homer and Duke came back inside, Homer said, "Zach, we've had some stress this mornin' 'cause we done ask a bunch of questions to fourteen deputies. Me and Tom need to sit down with ye to tell ye what we done found out. Tom took real good notes, but we promised Steven we'd give him a full report fer internal affairs. So, as soon as we git back, we'll talk 'bout it and ye can git to workin' on it. Ye can get Amelia to hep ye, if ye need to. This here's top priority 'cause we want internal affairs to git this guy and put him in the slammer."

Homer motioned for Brayden. When he walked over to him, Homer said, "Brayden, I want ye to fly back to Alabama fer a few days and check on my house, the bunkhouse, and especially check on Margaret and Mary Alice. Then come back as soon as ye can. Use your company credit card for the trip. Call me when ye git there and let me know if everything and everyone is okay. Be sure and stop at the florist before ye git to their house and take a nice bouquet to each lady. Say it is from all of us and we miss 'em."

"Got it, boss."

MEN IN BLACK

When the team arrived at the coffee shop, Homer introduced Tyler, Zach, Victoria, and Amelia. "This is our newest team member, Chief Deputy Sheriff Steven Adamson."

"It is a pleasure to meet everyone," Steven said, smiling.

"Homer and Tom are very impressed with you, Steven," Tyler remarked.

"Thanks. Homer, I have had an idea that I hope you and Tom like. I know you have rented a sailboat and have been on the Watauga River a few times, but I thought I might check into renting a tour bus so I can show everyone this beautiful area. You know we are in the mountains. We can take a nice weekend ride, and even walk a little on the Appalachian Trail, just to say we did. What do you say?"

"Looks like everybody likes the idea" Homer said. "Thar's only one thang."

"You'll not use your hard-earned money fer it. Have you done forgot that I've got over $5.2 million? You can use Tyler's credit card and we'll git you one ordered today," he added.

"Thanks, but let me do this and you can reimburse me later. Would that be okay with you?" Steven asked.

"I like somebody who's not afraid to argue with the boss," Homer said laughing. "That's fine. When do ye want to do this?"

"If I can get one rented, then this weekend is fine with me. Victoria, I was told that your parents are here. Please let them know that we want them to come with us," Steven said.

"That is very kind of you, Deputy Adamson," replied Victoria.

"Ok, then. I will let you know if I can reserve a tour bus for this weekend. I saw an advertisement recently for a rental car and tour bus company and they are right here in Boone. Tom, if you are available, would you mind going with me so we can try to rent one?"

"I don't mind. I'll be glad to go with you," responded Tom.

"Ok, let's git focused, guys. This is one of the toughest cases we've ever had. You know, our little Victoria was shot, and somebody done bugged our cabin, and we had two fake deputies on our front porch listening to everythang we've been sayin'. I think they did this to keep our mind off the case.

"I've done some thinkin' about this stuff. One thang we got sloppy on was we shoulda known rite off the bat these guys were fake deputies. We done gotta keep our eyes and ears open. Let's don't git sidetracked by sailboat rides or playing on the river. I promise we'll have plenty of time to do that when this case is closed." Homer wasn't smiling.

Steven commented that he was amazed at the level of deception and the attempt to cover up the guilty person in this murder investigation.

"To be honest," Homer began, "I think we're movin' along like we ought to. Stephanie's body was found and identified, we got a lot of evidence from her office, and now we know who was stealin' from the church and we got him arrested. Matthew is in the jailhouse fer killin' his wife. We done got the gun and silencer and we know who the deputy is who got Matthew's prints on them. We done got enough evidence on that crooked deputy that we can hand it over to internal affairs and let 'em run with it.

"What we don't got is the right man behind bars fer Stephanie's murder and we don't know who done shot Victoria. We don't know who put two fake deputies outside our cabin door fer awhile, or who put bugs in our cabin and stuff. We don't know what the reason was fer killing Stephanie, and we definitely don't know why we ain't caught that scum bag. So, as ye can see, we still got lots of work to do. We've got to catch the killer!"

"I know you are frustrated, Homer, but like you said at the beginning, we are progressing like we should. I have a feeling that we are going to know who the killer is very soon. Then we can collect all the evidence needed for the prosecutor to convince a jury, without a shadow of doubt, that the killer needs to be behind bars for a long, long time," said Tom.

"Thanks for the good word, Tom," Homer said.

"By the way, Deputy Adamson," Victoria began.

"Please, call me Steven."

"Ok, Steven," Victoria said with a smile. "My mom is an excellent cook, and she is setting another plate at the table tonight just for you. Can you join us? She is making homemade lasagna and salad," she said.

"Thanks, I'll be there. What are your parent's names?" Steven asked.

"Tommy and Peggy Owens."

"What time is dinner?" Steven asked.

"It's 'supper' in Alabama," laughed Tyler. "We usually eat at 6:00 p.m., but come early and stay late."

In the meantime, Matthew was in his cell getting more depressed over his predicament. As he laid back on his cot, he heard his cell being unlocked. He sat up quickly, but didn't recognize the deputy who walked in.

"I am Deputy Robert Smith, and I am assuming the position formerly held by Deputy Carpenter. He has been reassigned while criminal charges against him are pending. If you need anything, sir, just let me know. I have been instructed by Chief Deputy Adamson to show you utmost respect and that is what I intend to do," said the deputy.

"Seriously?" asked Matthew.

"Seriously, sir," replied the deputy. "Would you like to read a copy of today's newspaper? Also, Pastor

Henry White put money on your account, which means I can now bring you snacks or drinks. Do you want anything?"

"For real?" asked Matthew.

Deputy Smith laughed and replied, "Yes, seriously, sir."

"Wow! Then yes, I would like to have some chips and a coke. Is that possible? And, yes, I would like to read the newspaper. Thank you, Deputy Smith," Matthew said smiling.

"Yes, sir," Deputy Smith said, locking the cell as he left.

Chapter 15
An Unexpected Suspect

When they got back to the cabin, Tom and Homer met with Zach and updated him on the interviews at the sheriff's department. Tom handed him his notes and told him that he would be available if he had any questions.

Homer said, "See if ye can figger out what Tom done wrote down and then ye need to get that computer of yours and type out a copy fer Steven to git to internal affairs. Let me know when ye are done typing it 'cause I wanta read it before ye hand it off to Steven."

"I'll get right on it," Zach said, then headed to his room.

Early the next morning, Steven called Watauga Charter Bus Tours and Car Rentals in Boone. He asked if they had a tour bus available for Friday. The agent assured him they had a twenty-four-passenger bus if he was interested in that size.

"Yes, that's perfect," responded Steven.

"Would you like for me to reserve it for you?" the agent asked.

"Yes," he replied. He gave the agent the necessary information and informed him he would be in tomorrow to fill out the paperwork and pay the deposit.

Steven called Tom and told him he had reserved a tour bus and needed to go to the office. "If you are available tomorrow, I need your help driving one of the vehicles back to the cabin. Can you go with me? You can say no, if you'd like," Steven said.

AN UNEXPECTED SUSPECT

"I'm available and don't mind at all. On the way there, we can spend some time getting to know each other. After all, we will be teammates," Tom assured him.

The next day Steven arrived at the cabin to get Tom. "Tom and I are going to the rental company to reserve a tour bus for this Friday. Hopefully, it won't take long for us to get everything in order. We'll be back in a jiff!" Steven informed Homer.

As soon as they drove in the lot, a salesman greeted them asking if they came to buy an RV. "Sorry, sir, but we are here to reserve a tour bus. Can you show us the office where we are to sign in?" Tom asked.

"Yes, sir, you just stay straight and you'll see the office just ahead. Have a good day," the salesman told the men.

The office was easy to find. Tom found a parking place right in front. He decided to wait in the car while Steven finished the rental details.

Steven practically jumped out of the car he was so excited. He went inside, identified himself and gave the man behind the desk his confirmation number.

"Yes, sir, I have your papers ready if you'd like to look over them," the attendant said.

"I think I'll read it later," Steven said.

"I need a copy of your driver's license, insurance and payment method."

Steven was so eager to rent the tour bus and take the trip that he fumbled trying to get his wallet from his rear pocket. When he finally pulled it out of his pocket, he placed it on the counter. When he opened it, his Watauga

AN UNEXPECTED SUSPECT

County Chief Deputy Sheriff's badge was attached to the left side in plain sight.

The attendant said with excitement in his voice, "I saw the Watauga County Sheriff's badge displayed just like that when the sheriff rented a car from me a while back."

Trying not to look surprised and without looking up as he fumbled through his wallet, Steven asked, "Really? When was that?"

"Well, just a second and I'll tell you exactly," the attendant replied. "I feel pretty safe telling you since you are in law enforcement," he said laughing.

Steven produced his driver's license, insurance, and credit card as he waited on the attendant to give him a timeframe when the sheriff rented a car.

The attendant turned from his desk and put his book on the counter in front of Steven. "The sheriff rented a car on April 16th and returned it on April 18th of this year."

"Of course, that is when he and his brother went to visit family together. I'll tell him I met you when I get back to the office. Here are the things you needed from me," Steven said. "What time do we need to meet you here on Friday?"

"There is no need to come here, sir. Your tour bus driver will pick you up at your Cabin Rental Office at 7:00 a.m. Friday. Have a good day, and we hope you enjoy your tour," said the agent.

As soon as Steven got in the car, he immediately told Tom what had just happened in the office.

AN UNEXPECTED SUSPECT

"We need to tell Homer about this as soon as we get back to the cabin," Tom insisted.

When they got to the cabin, Brayden came driving up from his trip to Alabama. Steven was smiling when he parked beside Brayden's car. The three men made small talk on their way inside.

"Homer, we have something strange to report to you that we learned at the rental place," said Tom. "Would it be alright if we spoke in private? Perhaps on the porch? I'll let Steven tell you all about it."

"You bet. Let's go outside," Homer responded.

Steven told Homer about Sheriff Reed renting a car from the Watauga Charter Bus Tours and Car Rental where they rented the tour bus. He told Homer the car was rented in April for the exact timeframe as Stephanie's murder.

"Wow! The sheriff? For the same time that somebody killed Stephanie? Do ye think he dunit?" asked Homer.

"There is no reason that we should jump to conclusions," Steven said. "He has every right to do what he wants, and it is possible that he needed a certain kind of car that they had there. Let's not try to convict him just because we are eager to put the murderer behind bars. We should look into it though, without being obvious."

"Yep, good idea," Homer said.

Friday finally came and everyone was thrilled to take a tour of the area.

Brayden ran up to Homer and hugged him as he said, "You have been true to your word. Even though we have worked hard, you have made our off-time fun. Thank you for today!"

"Ok guys, git what ye need to take with ye. Cameras? Git a blanket in case ye git cold on the bus. We can stop fer lunch and supper on the road, but if you've got snacks, bring plenty to share. Tyler, did ye git a case of bottled water like I told ye?" Homer asked.

"Yes, sir."

"Mr. and Mrs. Owens, you go first, then Zach and Victoria. Everyone else, find a spot and enjoy yourselves," commented Steven.

They had traveled quite a distance when Amelia asked, "Homer, are you from North Carolina? Someone said that you were baptized in Matthew and Stephanie's church."

"My great-grandpappy, Bartlett Yancey, was born in what's now Yancey County. He was forty-seven years old in 1833, the year the county was named for him. He lived in North Carolina all his life and served in the North Carolina State Legislature, then was elected to the United States Congress. My grandpappy and my paw were raised in Yancey County, but when paw grew up, he moved to Blount County, Alabama, and that's where I was born. One time when we went back to visit family in Watauga County, we went to church at Hickory Grove Baptist Church, and I walked down that aisle, shook the preacher's hand and got baptized in Wilbur Lake. To this day, I don't know who Wilbur is. Now ye know my story, Amelia," Homer said with a laugh. "Another thang. I was so poor as a kid, I had a tumbleweed as a pet." Everyone laughed.

"Amelia, I was married, but lost her to cancer. We didn't have any kids. Thanks for asking about me!" Homer said.

"So, where are we going, Mr. Tour Guide?" asked Zach.

"Boone is in the Blue Ridge Mountains of the Appalachian Mountain Range. We are going to travel the entire 252 miles of the Blue Ridge Parkway in North Carolina. We will go to Asheville and tour the Biltmore House which was the main residence of George Vanderbilt between 1889 and 1895. It is the largest privately owned house in the United States with 178,926 square feet. It is still owed by the George Vanderbilt family," Steven answered.

"Now all of you know that this may have been my idea to rent this tour bus, but I am not going to be in charge of all the places we will go. Everyone can have input."

"For some reason, I'm remembering a trip we took when I was in high school, I think about an exchange student from way across the pond in Sweden who went with us. The teacher on the bus said, ' Now if anybody needs to stop to go to the bathroom, just be frank.' We'd been 'bout a hundred miles when the Swedish guy said, 'Mrs. McKinnon, I'm Frank'," Homer said. "Now ain't that funny?"

The team really enjoyed the time together touring the Appalachian Mountains of North Carolina on the Blue Ridge Parkway.

"Thank you, Steven, for planning this trip and for including Tommy and me," Peggy Owens said. "It was a trip we will never forget. I love to do scrapbooking and I can't wait to get my pictures together and get started."

Once back at the cabin, everyone helped unload the bus. Each one thanked Steven for a wonderful idea.

"I know it's late and everyone is tired. I am too, so I think I will head on home. See you tomorrow," Steven said. He waved goodbye and walked to his car.

"I'm exhausted from my trip back from Alabama and then going on our excursion today. I will give you a full report tomorrow if that's okay. I will say that Margaret and Mary Alice are doing fine and said to tell you they miss everyone. Is it okay if I head to bed?" Brayden asked Homer.

"Sure, and thanks, fer checking on Margaret and Mary Alice fer me. I'm glad you're back. We missed you.

Night, Brayden. We'll see ye bright and early at breakfast," Homer said.

During breakfast, Brayden opened the conversation. "Alabama is still beautiful, and it was good to sleep in my own bed in the bunkhouse. I had a meal or two with Margaret and Mary Alice. For their ages, I thought they were doing great. They walk everyday like they have for several years, and they watch *Gun Smoke* every night. So, overall, I'd say they are healthy and enjoying life. They do miss us! Homer, they gave me a message for you," Brayden said.

"Really, what did they say?" Homer asked.

"They want you to check in once in a while!" Brayden said with a grin.

"Okay, okay, I will." Homer replied. "I miss 'em, too."

Homer's phone rang. "This is Homer."

"Hello, is this Homer Yancey?" asked the man.

"Yes, what can I do fer ye?" asked Homer.

"My name is Paul Franklin, and I'm a neighbor of Matthew Wright's. I'm a retired Atlanta Police Officer and I was wondering if we could meet?" the gentleman asked.

"Sure, any time. Where ye wanta meet?" Homer asked.

"If you want to come to my house, we can speak in private here or if you prefer, I can come to you — your choice," Mr. Franklin said.

"Ye can come here? We're at the Daniel Boone Park in Cabin 17. Can ye be here at 10 a.m.?" Homer asked.

"Thank you, Mr. Yancey. I'll be there." Mr. Franklin ended the call.

What was that all about, Homer?" asked Tom.

"It was a guy named Franklin. Paul, I think. He said he's retired from the Atlanta Police Department and he lives in Matthew's neighborhood. I know what ye are going to say, Tom. We need to be careful since we had fake deputies we thought were guarding us. Tom, that's why he's coming here to talk. We all need to be here when he comes. Amelia, I'd like for ye to take notes of the meeting. Let's all stay alert, too, and make sure he's legit. We can even ask to see his ID if ye like that idea, Tom?" Homer asked.

AN UNEXPECTED SUSPECT

"I definitely think it is appropriate. Did he say why he wanted to meet with you?" Tom asked.

"He didn't tell me, but it sounded like he had somethang important to say. Maybe he has some information fer us 'bout Matthew or something he saw," Homer said.

"How is Matthew, anyhow? Do ye think by now he knows that Deputy Carpenter ain't in charge of the jail?" asked Homer.

"I imagine that either Steven or the new jailer told him." Tom answered.

"I think I'll take Duke outside fer a minute before Mr. Franklin gits here. Thanks fer the grits and eggs, Mrs. Owens. They was real good," Homer said as Duke pulled him out the door.

When they came inside, Zach handed Homer the first draft of the answers given by the deputies during Yancey Investigative Services' internal investigation.

"Please review what I have written, Homer. Maybe you and Tom can look it over and let me know what revisions I might need to make. I know you promised this report as soon as possible so Steven can give it to internal affairs. Here, I even brought a red pen so you can mark it up if you find mistakes or need to add something," Zach said.

"Thanks, Zach. I know a lot of hard work went into this report and we appreciate your attention to detail. Homer and I will review it together after lunch," Tom said. 'Don't worry, it won't be too bloody with red pen marks when we hand it back!"

AN UNEXPECTED SUSPECT

Homer picked up the daily newspaper and sat in the recliner in the living room. He was asleep within ten minutes.

"Don't anyone wake Homer. I think he has lost sleep ever since Matthew was arrested. Let's at least let him rest until 9:45 a.m.," Tom told the team.

The team members all gave a thumbs up.

Mr. Franklin was seen parking his car in front of the cabin about five minutes before his appointment. Tom walked over to Homer and gently touched his arm. When he did, Homer sat straight up and asked, "What time is it? Is MacFayden here yet?"

"He's parking his car, Homer." Tom said.

"I'm up!" Homer said while stretching.

|335|

"Buddy! Go brush your teeth!" Tom said waving his hand in front of his face.

"Sorry," Homer said and rushed down the hall to his room.

Moments later, Homer reappeared to see Mr. Franklin talking to Tom and other team members in the living room.

Homer extended his hand to the gentleman and said, "I'm Homer Yancey, what can I do fer ye?"

Chapter 16
Watchful Eyes

"Nice to meet you, Mr. Yancey." He reached into his wallet and pulled out his ID. Just to show you I'm not some kind of kook, this shows that I retired from the Atlanta Police Department. I was a detective and held the rank of lieutenant on the force, as you can read on the card."

Homer looked carefully at the card and handed it back to Mr. Franklin. "What can I do fer ye?"

"Mr. Yancey, the day that you and several others drove into Whispering Woods Subdivision, I was working in my front yard. By the number of law enforcement officers, I assumed you were there with a search warrant. I also saw your colleagues congratulating you when everyone left. That told me that you found what you were there to locate.

"Mr. Yancey, the reason that I am here today is not to get into your business, but I do have information that you might find rather interesting. I have struggled whether I should tell you, but I just can't let go of my detective training, so here I am.

"I found it strange that about an hour before you entered Matthew's house with the search warrant, the sheriff drove in Matthew's driveway and then entered the house. He was carrying a plastic bag. I guess no one else would have recognized it as an evidence bag. He was in Matthew's house less than ten minutes, and when he exited, I did not see him carrying the evidence bag. Now, it could have been in his pocket, or at least in his possession, but I did not see it.

"When the sheriff pulled out of the driveway, I turned my back like I was oblivious to what was going on at Matthew's house. Mr. Yancey, I do think I smell a rat," Mr. Franklin said.

"Mr. Franklin, would you be willing to testify if called upon to tell a jury what you just told us?" asked Zach.

"Absolutely. Not because Matthew is my neighbor, but I think it looks suspicious for the sheriff to come alone and briefly go into Matthew's house. In my opinion, its unusual behavior. I know I'm rambling, but I think the sheriff may have stepped outside the law," Mr. Franklin said with a serious expression.

Homer started pacing and scratching his head. He stopped and turned towards Mr. Franklin. "Sir, thank ye fer having the courage to come here and fer tellin' us what ye saw. It's a real help to us, and ye just give us a big ole piece that fits rite into our puzzle. Thank ye. If ye think of anythang else, I need ye to call me. Here's my card, and if you can't git me, call Tom Lynch. Tom, give him your card, too. Would you please leave your address and phone number with Tyler in case we have additional questions? Tyler take his information," Homer said and thanked Mr. Franklin. The gentleman left.

"Tyler, I want ye and Brayden to go to the Whispering Woods neighborhood and talk to some other folks that might have saw somethang. If ye can git two of 'em to say the same thang Mr. Franklin done said, then we've got ourself a lead. Ye guys get a move on 'cause what Mr. Franklin said he done saw could help us nail a murderer. We need to make sure Mr. Franklin is right before we can tell a prosecutor. I think it would be smart to see just where Mr. Franklin lives to make sure he can see what could of happened at Matthew's house. Ye guys got detective licenses; ye know what to do, so go do it," Homer said with urgency.

Brayden grabbed his notebook and laptop, then came back into the living room. "Homer, thanks for giving us this assignment. We won't disappoint you." He and Tyler hurried out the door, got into Brayden's car, and drove away.

About thirty minutes later, Brayden and Tyler continued down Cove Circle and made a note that from Mr. Franklin's house, he could easily see activity at Matthew's. The location of his house gave credibility to Mr. Franklin's story. As they slowly drove down the road, they saw three homes with people working in their yards. They stopped at the first house.

Before getting out of the car, Tyler told Brayden that the mailbox sign indicated that the Fowlers lived there.

As they got out of the car, Tyler introduced himself to the couple in the front yard and then introduced Brayden. They explained that they worked for Yancey Investigative Services. Once the couple heard they were hired to investigate the murder of Stephanie Wright, they were eager to help.

"We have known Matthew and Stephanie for several years and really find it hard to believe he could have killed his wife. He adored her, and for all appearances, they had a happy marriage." Mr. Fowler said. "We miss Stephanie. We used to get together occasionally and have a cookout during the summer. I'm sorry for babbling. Please, what can we do for you, gentlemen?"

"We were wondering if you happened to be home when the sheriff deputies came to search Matthew's house and property?" asked Brayden.

WATCHFUL EYES

"Yes, we were working in the front yard that day. As I remember, the sheriff came to the house about an hour before everyone else arrived, but he stayed only about ten minutes. Later, there were lots of cops that went into Matthew's house. They must have found what they were searching for, because they all seemed pretty cheerful when they came out," Mr. Fowler continued.

"Would you be willing to testify in court regarding what you just told us, if called to do so?" asked Tyler.

"I don't know what I just said that made you think it was helpful to your investigation, but, yes, I'll agree to testify," Mr. Fowler said. He reached in his pocket and retrieved his business card and handed it to Tyler.

"Here's my card if you need to get in touch with me. I own an air-conditioning company in town. Things get busy for us this time of year, however, just call the number on that card and I will answer," Mr. Fowler instructed.

"Thank you for taking our questions. We'll be in touch. By the way, your yard looks amazing. Have a nice day," Brayden said.

"Thanks, my wife decided to plant two new shrubs this year and guess who dug up the old ones to make room for the new ones? Anyway, I believe her new choice is much better than the old one," he said as he walked over to the shrub which was full of pink blossoms.

When they got back in the car, Brayden said, "It's nice when people aren't intimidated by investigators and are willing to take a few minutes to answer questions. That couple seemed really friendly."

"Yeah, I agree. Let's see the next couple that live within a few houses of Matthew. Perhaps they saw something the day we had the search warrant. Look, the couple is still working in their yard. Tyler, there's no name on the mailbox."

When they got out of the car, Tyler extended his hand to the man and introduced both he and Brayden and told him they worked for Yancey Investigative Services.

"I'm Bryant Simmons," the man introduced himself, "and this is my wife, Leah."

Leah stepped forward and offered the men lemonade and a seat on their front porch, which extended the length of their house and had an unobstructed view of Matthew's house.

Brayden and Tyler eagerly accepted both offers and sat, then posed the same questions they had asked the Fowlers.

The couple was asked the same questions as the Fowlers. Mr. Simmons said, "About an hour before the rest of the cops came to Matthew's house, the sheriff drove up, then went inside, but only stayed maybe ten minutes. The reason I know it was the sheriff is because, his name was written on the side of his car. Also, I have seen him on television a lot. Yes, it was the sheriff. Anyway, he came later with the rest of the cops when they searched Matthew's house."

Brayden thanked the couple for the lemonade, their hospitality and for answering their questions. They also agreed to testify if needed. Brayden wrote down their names, address, and Mr. Simmons cell phone number.

WATCHFUL EYES

Back in the car, Tyler commented, "I think we should interview one more couple on this street. What do you think, Brayden?"

"That sounds good to me. We can then go back to the cabin and give Homer a report. Do you think he'll offer us lemonade, too?" Brayden answered with a laugh.

The last couple was walking inside their house as Brayden drove into their driveway. The lady saw them and walked back outside. "Hello, may I help you?" she asked just as her husband came back outside.

The man said with a stern expression, "If you're selling something, I ain't buying!"

Tyler said, "No sir, we aren't selling anything. I'm Tyler Frye and this is Brayden Davis. We work for Yancey

Investigative Services, and we were hired to investigate the murder of Stephanie Wright."

"I apologize, gentlemen, for being rude to you when you drove up. We get so many people on this block trying to sell us stuff that it's making me grumpy. As to Stephanie's death, it really makes us sad. We really like Matthew. If there is anything we can do for him, we're willing. How is he?" the man asked.

"Oh, again, please forgive my rudeness! I'm Adam Nunley and this is my wife, Martha," he said and extended his hand. After the handshakes, he repeated his question. "How is Matthew?"

"He is doing pretty good. We are trying to gather evidence to hopefully prove his innocence. Do you mind if we ask you a few questions?" asked Tyler.

"I'd be glad to answer your questions if I can," he responded.

"Were you home the day that law enforcement came to search Matthew's house?" asked Brayden.

"Yes, we were both working in our yard. It seems everyone in this neighborhood loves to do that. To me it isn't a lot of fun to get all sweaty over a blade of grass," he said. His wife elbowed him in his side.

"Do you remember anything unusual that caught your attention that day?" asked Tyler.

"Yes, as a matter of fact, I do remember something unusual. The sheriff drove up in front of Matthew's about an hour or so before everyone else came. I know it was him because I have seen him on television a lot. It was definitely the sheriff. I don't know if that detail matters to you. Anyway, he went into Matthew's house but only stayed inside a few minutes, then left. A lot of fuzz, sorry, I meant cops, showed up an hour or so later with what I assume was a search warrant. There must have been a dozen or more cops. I guess they found whatever it was they were looking for because when they came back outside, it looked like they were congratulating the man who found it. Now that is just speculation on my part," Mr. Simmons explained.

Tyler asked him if he would be willing to testify if he were called. He first said, "No." At least that was his answer until his wife hit him again in his ribs with her elbow. He then said, "Let me rephrase that. I would be glad to testify if needed," he said with a grin.

"Thank you both for taking the time today to tell us what you saw, and for agreeing to testify if needed. I hope both of you have a great rest of the day. Here is my business card, in the event you have anything to add or if you have questions. It was really nice to have met you," Brayden said. He and Tyler got in his car and started to leave.

Suddenly, Mr. Simmons ran towards Brayden's car waving his hand in the air, motioning for him to stop. Brayden hit the brakes. Mr. Simmons came around the car to Brayden's window.

"Mr. Davis, I'm sorry to flag you down like that, but I already have a question. "Do you think my testimony would be helpful to Matthew if I'm called? I only told you that I saw the sheriff go into Matthew's house. Please explain to me how my testimony would help," Mr. Simmons sincerely asked.

Brayden and Tyler got out of the car. Brayden said, "You take this one, Tyler."

"Mr. Simmons, witnesses are a critical part of criminal trials. Strong testimony from even one good witness can sometimes make or break the prosecution's case. Other than expert witnesses — who give opinions on specialized knowledge like forensics and DNA evidence — witnesses testify about what they've seen or heard. The personal testimony of one witness can be so persuasive to juries. Sometimes, witness testimony is the only evidence that gives a clear picture of what happened at the scene of the crime. Mr. Simmons, this is why we asked you ahead of the trial if you would be willing to testify. Thank you for agreeing and for your cooperation," Tyler said.

"Thank you for explaining that to me. It doesn't seem intimidating when I know it will help Matthew.

Again, thanks for the explanation, and I hope you have a great day," Mr. Simmons said as he backed away from Brayden's car.

Since the Simmons were the last to be interviewed, the men drove back to the cabin. They were eager to give their report to Homer and then do some fishing.

Back at the cabin, they immediately spotted Homer with a fishing rod in his hand walking towards the Watauga River. Brayden rolled down his window and shouted, "May we join you, Homer?"

"Come on, we can fish while ye tell me what happened when ye were fishing for evidence," Homer said. "Now that was funny as all git out, don't ye think? Sometimes I just slay myself." he said while laughing.

"I want ye fellas to type up everthang that the folks said today when ye asked 'em stuff and if they'd testify if we need 'em. Whatever ye type up, git it as near word fer word as ye can, then have 'em sign and date it. Divide up this assignment, guys. When you're done typing it, please let Tom look at it before ye git it signed. Good work today, guys," Homer said.

"Thanks, Homer. Everyone we interviewed today was polite and cooperative."

"Oh, somethang else, I'd like to git the real names of the fake deputies, and the name of the jerk who paid 'em. Ask Tom how you can git that information," Homer said.

Tom had been sitting on the porch watching Brayden, Tyler and Homer discussing something down by the river. He decided to join them.

WATCHFUL EYES

"Hi Tom. We were just wondering how we can git the real names of the fake deputies that spied on us and who hired 'em," Homer explained.

"Homer, Mrs. Owens has lunch ready," Tom said.

The men walked back to the cabin where they could further discuss the case.

"I think we just need to call the FBI headquarters here, identify ourselves, and find out who was Assigned to do surveillance on our cabin. We should have already been given that information, but there is no reason why we can't ask for it," answered Tom.

"Then let's git 'er done. Tom, you got a good strong voice and ye got more learnin' than me, so ye need to be the one to call. Ye okay with that? We need answers, don't ye think?" asked Homer.

"Sure, right after lunch, if that's okay," Tom replied.

There was a knock on the door. It was the sheriff.

Chapter 17
Research Uncovers Clue

"I just came by to see if everything's okay. How's the investigation coming along? I haven't seen much of you guys lately, which I hope means that you have wrapped things up since the killer is in jail. Last night I was thinking about how the forensic report said **the murderer gave Stephanie a powerful blow to the back of her neck** and shot her in the head at close range. I know this is your investigation, but I was wondering why he did both. Matthew may never give us an answer to that question, but it's strange, don't you think?" asked Sheriff Reed.

"Yeah, we might never know. That's a plum good question, sheriff. I think I'll ask **Matthew** that myself, or have the prosecutor ask **him that question** at his trial," Homer commented.

"We're fixin' to eat lunch. Want a plate and sit a spell, sheriff?" asked Homer.

"Thanks, but I have tons of work to do at the office. I just thought I would pay a friendly visit to you guys. If it's okay, I'll take a raincheck. If I can help in anyway, please don't hesitate to call me. Good to see you guys," the sheriff said and shook hands with Homer and Tom before leaving.

After the sheriff drove away, Homer said, "Do ye know what I reckon **is** strange 'bout his visit, Tom?"

"What?" asked Tom.

"How did he know somebody hit her in the back of the neck and that she got shot in the head?" Homer replied. "That thar forensic report was only sent to us, so how did he know all that?"

RESEARCH UNCOVERS CLUE

"Good question. How did he know? We need to ask Steven if the sheriff got a copy of the forensic report. Either way, we need to take note of this," Tom replied.

"But before it slips my mind, we oughta call the FBI Field Office here in North Carolina and ask for those two guys from the FBI who done come here and took 'em two fake deputies away. I wanna know who hired 'em. I think the men's names were Rutledge and Todd. Nobody ever answered that question. Tom, do ye know how to git the FBI's phone number?" asked Homer.

"Sure, all I have to do is go on the internet and find it. Just a minute and I'll do that on my phone," Tom replied.

"You need to learn me how to do fancy stuff like that sometime," Homer said.

"Ok, here's the number," Tom said as he wrote it down for Homer and handed it to him.

Homer told Tom that when the agents got on the line for him to do the talking. Homer called the number. He put his phone on speaker so Tom could hear.

"Federal Bureau of Investigation. How may I direct your call?"

"I need to speak to Agent Ron Rutledge, please," Homer requested.

"One moment, please."

Several moments later the operator said, "Sir, there is not an agent here by that name. Are you certain you have the right name?"

"May I speak with Agent Jeff Todd?"

RESEARCH UNCOVERS CLUE

"One moment, please."

"Excuse me sir, again, there is no agent at the FBI with that name. I'm sorry, sir," she said, then ended the call.

"Ye done kidding me, Tom? Did ye hear that woman? What in thunder is goin' on?" asked Homer.

"Now let's not panic. We had both wondered how the men guarding us could have been in Watauga County sheriff's deputy uniforms if they didn't work for the department. Who would have supplied them with uniforms?" Tom asked.

"Well, I gest thought of somethang else. Brayden called the North Carolina FBI to see if those two guys who said they was FBI were fer real. Did he call the wrong number? Did the FBI lie to him?" Homer suggested.

"Let's just ask Brayden to come in here with us for a few minutes and to bring his phone. I think he and Tyler are working on the witness document in Tyler's room. I'll get him," Tom said.

In just a few minutes Brayden came into the living room and sat across from Homer. "Need something, boss?" he asked.

"Look on your phone and give me the number ye called to check if them two FBI guys were fer real," Homer instructed.

Brayden found the number he called and wrote it down for Homer. Homer called the number.

"We're sorry. This is not a working number." The recording said. Homer called again and got the same recording.

RESEARCH UNCOVERS CLUE

Brayden reminded Homer that the agents were taking the deputies they arrested as imposters to the Boone Police Department. "Why not call and see if that happened?" Brayden suggested.

Homer called the number. "Boone Police Department."

"May I talk to the chief? This is Homer Yancey with Yancey Investigative Services."

"One moment, Mr. Yancey."

"Homer, good to hear from you. How can I be of help, today?" the chief asked.

Homer told the chief his concerns about the FBI agents and the uniformed deputies and asked if he could make any sense of it.

The chief responded, "I am assuming you are about to solve not only Mrs. Wright's murder, but you must be zeroing in on someone pretty powerful. Homer, watch your back all the time.

"To answer your question, 'Yes,' two men were brought here by two men identifying themselves as FBI agents. We learned that the two men were in fact imposters hired to put listening devices in your cabin and report your coming and goings. They don't know who hired them, and the judge has informally told us to keep them until they tell us who and why they were hired. As far as the agents, they are legitimate, but were instructed to give you false names. We have their real identities. Agent Frank MacFayden and Agent Nick Washburn. They are out of the North Carolina FBI Field Office. I have no idea how or why they got involved in the murder of Stephanie Wright."

"Thanks for your help, chief. The names you just gave us will help a lot. I'll keep in touch. Stay safe," Homer said and ended the call.

After relating to Tom and Brayden the details of the call with the chief, Homer called the FBI again.

"Federal Bureau of Investigation. How may I direct your call?"

"I would like to speak to Agent Frank MacFayden, please.

"One moment, please."

"Hello, this is Agent MacFayden. May I help you?"

"Yes, this is Homer Yancey with Yancey Investigative Services. Remember me? Ye came to my cabin in Boone and hauled two county deputies away and charged them with impersonating an officer. Does that ring a bell, sir?"

"Yes, sir. I apologize for giving you a false name. We are also surveilling someone which should help you with your investigation in the murder of Stephanie Wright," he said.

"We didn't call ye. What makes ye have the notion we want the FBI snooping around in our business?" Homer asked.

"As a peace offering, sir, I will tell you that these two men were not deputies but were hired by Sheriff Reed to listen to your conversations and report your daily whereabouts," the agent said.

"Is thar anythang else we need to know?" Homer asked.

RESEARCH UNCOVERS CLUE

Sir, if it is okay with you, I can meet you at the coffee shop where you meet with Chief Deputy Adamson. I'm the guy that sits in the booth across from you with a computer and a cup of coffee. Sorry sir, those were my instructions," he explained.

Homer was getting pretty irritated. "I'm 'bout to fly off the handle, young man. I'll meet ye in the mornin' at 10:00 o'clock sharp at the coffee shop." Homer hung up.

"Tom. Let's go rent a van and then take a ride. We can call the Watauga Charter Bus Tours and Car Rental and see if they have one available," Homer said.

"Let me go outside and make the call. I will look up the number," Tom said as he walked outside.

"Hello, do you have a Mercedes passenger van available for rent?" asked Tom. "What is the seating capacity?"

"The Mercedes Sprinter Passenger van seats twelve," the rental agent answered.

"Is it available today? We can be there in two hours. Will that work for you?" asked Tom. "Great, see you soon. I am Tom Lynch."

"Okay, Homer. Let's go. We have to be at the rental company within two hours in order to get the van. We will both have to drive vehicles back here, so we don't leave our car there," Tom said.

"Let's roll," Homer said. "Brayden, we're leaving will be back soon. We'll take the stuff you gave me and we'll read it on the way. I'll call ye with an okay or with any changes," Homer said. "Tell Mrs. Owens we won't be eatin' supper here tonight. Thanks."

Meanwhile, at North Carolina State University in Raleigh, North Carolina, a research student by the name of Paul Castile was researching the number of individuals currently in the state of North Carolina who were dishonorably discharged from the military. He learned that North Carolina is home to around 700,000 veterans.

He also learned that a dishonorable discharge is reserved for crimes such as murder, manslaughter, sexual assault, and desertion. Those who receive a dishonorable discharge lose all of their military benefits and are forbidden from owning firearms as civilians. Paul also discovered there are currently eight-five veterans in North Carolina who received a military dishonorable discharge.

After compiling a list of the names of the eighty-five North Carolina residents holding a dishonorable discharge, Paul decided to research where these men are currently.

As he continued his research, he learned that twenty-seven of these veterans had died, nineteen were World War II disabled veterans, fourteen were currently in nursing homes, seven were in federal prison, the whereabouts of six was unknown, five were retired and now over the age of seventy-five, and seven are listed as presently in the workforce and paying federal income tax.

Because these men were in the workforce and paying taxes, he was curious as to the whereabouts of these men.

RESEARCH UNCOVERS CLUE

He had one main goal with all his researching — to make a good grade! He was not only intrigued by his research topic and what he had learned so far, but now he was driven to outline a methodical approach as to the whereabouts of these seven men. Had they been able to hold good jobs or were they living a life of despair of their own making?

Bingo! *Allan Thomas Reed living in Boone, North Carolina is currently serving as sheriff of Watauga County.* The facts about Mr. Reed prompted Paul to ask his professor for advice on what to do with the information.

Paul met with Professor Chambers at the end of the day. "Professor, in my research regarding military dishonorably discharged individuals in North Carolina, I discovered data regarding one individual who is currently serving as a county sheriff. A person with this type of discharge is prohibited from owning or carrying a firearm. Obviously, a sheriff carries a firearm. What do you suggest I do with this material other than include it in my research paper?" Paul asked.

"Mr. Castile, I recommend you do further research on this individual before hastily notifying him of your findings, or reporting him to someone higher in command," Professor Chambers suggested. "My other recommendation is that you verify your information. Your information certainly sounds intriguing, but it is of little use in your research paper if your information is not verified," Professor Chambers said.

"For example, you may find your research to be questionable if told that dishonorable discharge information is confidential. In reality, this evidence is considered public data through the Register of Deeds or by submitting Form

RESEARCH UNCOVERS CLUE

180 to the National Personnel Records Center," the professor explained.

Paul thanked the professor and left.

Since it was the weekend, Paul decided to drive to Boone and do further research on Sheriff Allan Thomas Reed. When he arrived in Boone, he saw a sign advertising cabins for rent at the Daniel Boone Park.

At the park reservation office, Paul was able to afford three nights at a college student's reduced rate. After using his credit card, the attendant gave him the keys to Cabin Sixteen. The attendant whispered to Paul, "You will be next door to a famous detective here investigating a high-profile murder case. I think his team is working with our local sheriff."

An hour later, Tom drove the Mercedes van into the park, followed by Homer in his SUV. They both parked in front of the cabin. Paul peeked out his window to see who drove past his cabin. He watched two men enter Cabin 17.

Paul said to himself, "Tomorrow, I'll introduce myself and tell them why I am here. Maybe I'll get to meet the famous detective."

Tom and Homer came inside the cabin. Homer said, "I'd like to have a short team meeting."

It was only 7 p.m. Most of the team were either watching television or reading.

"Tyler, would ye call everbody into the living room so I can tell ye what's up?"

"Sure, boss," Tyler replied as he headed down the hallway.

RESEARCH UNCOVERS CLUE

About five minutes later, every team member was accounted for.

"Okay, we have some thangs to talk 'bout and 'cause we don't need nobody listening, Tom and I went and rented a van so we can meet without no durn ease droppers. Let's go outside," Homer instructed.

When everyone was inside the van, it was Zach who said, "Homer, you sure believe in doing things right. This is really nice. Did you notice that each van seat has a tray in the arm just like on airplanes? That sure makes it easy for us to take notes. Also, I like the dark tinted windows. Nice touch, Homer."

"Are ye done drooling, Zach?" Homer asked with a grin.

"There's still more thangs we've left danglin.' One, I think it was the sheriff we think done put 'em in the nightstand beside Matthew's bed. I know, we can't assume, we have to prove.

"Two, we have some folks who live on Cove Circle that seen the sheriff go in Matthew's house 'bout an hour before we all got thar with the search warrant. All the neighbors our team talked to said the sheriff was only there 'bout ten minutes, which was long enough to put the gun and silencer in the **nightstand**. The neighbors who seen the sheriff that day are willing to testify in court, if needed.

"Three, the Forensic Auditing Services helped us to find the guy who was stealin' from the church. Rex Smith is sittin' in a jail cell tonight fer stealing $17,000.

"Four, we learnt that the two deputies who were on our porch acting like guards were not real lawmen. They were handcuffed and took to the Boone Police Department and are now sittin' in jail and are charged with impersonating an officer of the law. They confessed that Sheriff Reed hired 'em. The chief told us that he's gonna keep these guys locked up 'till they squeal like a cat who got its tail stepped on. He wants to know <u>why</u> they was hired.

"Five, we heard straight from the sheriff's mouth the other day when he was here that, and I quote:

> 'Last night I was thinking about how the forensic report said that Matthew inflicted a hard blow in the back of Stephanie's neck and he shot her in the head at close range. I know this is your investigation, but I was wondering why he did both. Matthew may never give us an answer to that question, but it's strange, don't you think?'

Homer quoted from what he had written in his notebook.

"Six, we're gonna meet with a real FBI Agent in the mornin'," Homer said.

Chapter 18
The Engagement

Homer continued telling the team with whom they would be meeting at the Coffee Shop.

"We're gonna see one of them FBI guys who done came here, hauled them two fake deputies off to jail, found them durn bugs and took 'em all out of the cabin, and then made us all madder than a wet hen when they done give us phony names. Now, folks, that dog don't hunt with me.

"Steven, it's lookin' more and more like our killer is none other than your dadburn boss. If it's the sheriff, he's 'bout as worthless as gum on a boot heel. We've gotta prove it faster than a hot knife through butter, 'cause we ain't got Stephanie's real killer behind bars yet.

"Rite now, I feel about as useful as a trapdoor in a canoe. The gun that killed Stephanie ain't registered and the silencer ain't either. So, detectives, if the killer is the sheriff, my question is this," Homer said. "where and how did a sheriff who is sworn to uphold the dad-blamed law git an unregistered gun and an illegal silencer? Another thang that keeps me up at night is why he done killed her. I just don't git it. Why would a sheriff want to kill a church secretary? And besides that, who in blazes shot Victoria and why?

"The main reason that I wanted to rent this here van is 'cause I ain't shore there ain't no more bugs in the cabin. Me and Tom wanted a safe place to meet. Like I said, there are still things we just don't know. I stay awake at night 'cause my brain's rattlin' around like a BB in a boxcar trying to figger all this out. This here's been the strangest case we've ever done took on. Ye have worked real hard and are good detectives. We all want answers. Keep thinking of questions and we'll come back here tomorrow

THE ENGAGEMENT

nite. In the mornin,' let's not talk 'bout this stuff with Steven or the agent. We just need to see what that blame FBI **guy** has to say. Night, folks," Homer said. "I'm plum tuckered out. I'm gonna take Duke for a walk, then we can hit the sack."

"Homer, I sure am glad you brought Duke with us on this trip. If it wasn't for Duke, we might still be looking for Stephanie's grave. I think he's getting a little restless. Do you think he feels left out?" asked Zach.

"I reckon you could be right. He and I do a lot of thangs together at home, and he gits pretty spoilt. I done been so busy here that he's been pretty lonely. Maybe we could all play with him more," said Homer.

"Not a problem. We all like Duke," Zach said. "Good night, Homer. Good night, Duke."

Duke barked and wagged his tail when he heard his name.

The next morning, Paul Castile was disappointed when he saw the Yancey team leave in the van. He decided to explore more on Sheriff Reed until the team returned.

"I wonder if the sheriff was ever married," Paul asked himself. He opened his computer, took another sip of coffee, and started his research.

Because Paul immensely enjoyed research, he chose to attend North Carolina State University. NCSU was known for being one of the three major research universities that make up the Research Triangle.

Paul had struggled regarding a career to pursue after graduation. He was glad he had time to think and pray away from the campus. His cabin was a perfect setting for researching the information he needed to make a good grade. As he gazed out the window in deep thought, he said to himself,

> *This research just helped me realize something. This is the kind of work I think I want to do as a career.*
>
> *Actually, I think I'd like to do investigative research at a military research installation!*
>
> *I think I'll call Mom and Dad and tell them I finally made up my mind. Then I'll call my professor with the good news!*
>
> *Thank you, Sheriff Allan Reed, for helping me to make my career decision."*

Before moving on with a job search, he knew he needed to stay focused on Sheriff Reed and whether he had ever been married.

After studying for several hours, going deeper and deeper into the life of Watauga County Sheriff Allan Reed, Paul learned that although he never married, he was once engaged to Stephanie Lynn Hicks. The timeframe of their engagement ending appeared to be shortly after Allan Reed was dishonorably discharged.

"I wonder why she didn't stand by her man?" Paul asked himself. "I think I'll look for an answer."

Paul looked into more information on Allan Reed. His dishonorable discharge was handed down for what the military considers the most reprehensible conduct. His inquiries revealed that this type of discharge could only have been rendered by conviction at a general court-martial for a serious offense. Sheriff Reed was convicted of sexual assault that called for a dishonorable discharge as part of the sentence.

THE ENGAGEMENT

In addition, Paul learned that those who receive a dishonorable discharge lose all of their military benefits and are forbidden from receiving or possessing firearms.

Paul decided that he would share this information with his next-door neighbor, Mr. Yancey. He was certain that Mr. Yancey would like to know about the sheriff because for all he knew, Mr. Yancey was working with the sheriff on a murder investigation. Paul didn't know if Mr. Yancy would be interested in knowing that the sheriff was engaged once.

While Paul was researching information on Sheriff Allan Reed, the team met Steven Adamson and FBI Agent Nick Washburn at the coffee shop.

"Steven, this is FBI Agent Nick Washburn. He's one of the agents who grabbed the two men who faked it as deputies and then took 'em into the Police Department and had 'em arrested. Don't it just git ye fired up when ye think 'bout them guys spying on us? We've learnt from the police chief that the men confessed that Sheriff Reed hired them.

"Steven, it's shore looking more and more like the sheriff has got his fingers all in this mess. I have a bunch of clues that point rite in his direction.

"Agent Washburn told me he's been sittin' at the table across from us here every day listenin' to everythang we've been saying. I got him to come so we could ask him some questions," said Homer.

"I've got a question, Agent Washburn," said Steven with irritation in his voice. "Why in heaven's name does the FBI think they have the right to take over our investigation?"

THE ENGAGEMENT

"Sir, I understand your frustration, but I can assure you that the sheriff's department and Yancey Investigative Services are not outranked by the FBI and we will not supervise or take over your investigation. It is my understanding, sir, that a good friend of Mr. Yancey's, Alabama Governor Brett McKinney, contacted North Carolina Governor Robert Burns and requested the FBI's investigative resources be made available if needed.

"Before identifying Agent Brian MacFayden and myself, we observed two men in deputy uniforms standing nightly by your front door. We believed they were there for your protection until we saw them using listening devices to eavesdrop on your conversations. This occurred for several nights, which is why we apprehended them and turned them over to the Boone Police Department to be charged with impersonating an officer. We were under orders from Governor Burns not to identify ourselves until we were certain of your safety.

"Sir, I believe the FBI's investigative resources can be helpful if you choose to allow us to assist in solving this case," the agent said.

"I assume you are aware that we believe we have identified Stephanie's murderer?" asked Steven.

"Yes," replied Agent Washburn, who knew these men did not like the FBI's involvement in their case.

"We'll do our best to help you, sir. Thank you. Please call me Nick," the agent responded.

"Another thang, Nick. You and Brian plan on coming fer supper tonight to meet the whole team and sink your teeth into the best home cookin' you've had in a long time. See you at 6:00 p.m. sharp." Homer said, then shook Nick's hand.

"I sure you sensed the irritation in my voice. I apologize. I know you did the right thing, Homer. I guess it made me upset that the FBI showed up unannounced for what I assumed was a takeover of our investigation. I guess that shows I'm prideful of our abilities. For that, I'm sorry," confessed Steven.

"Let's just take all the hep we can git. If the sheriff done it, let's have him see what the inside of a cell is like and put the rascal in the slammer fer a long, long time," Homer said.

"Absolutely. I'll see you at 6:00 p.m. for supper," Steven said with a grin.

About 5:00 p.m., Paul noticed that the whole Yancey team seemed to be at the cabin, so he decided to take his computer and meet the team.

There was a knock on the door. When Brayden answered the door, a young man said, "Please allow me to introduce myself. I am Paul Castile, a research student at NC State and I have rented Cabin 16 for a few days."

Brayden shook hands with Paul and introduced himself. "Won't you come in and meet everyone?"

"If I'm not interrupting anything, I would like that. Thanks," Paul said.

After the introductions, Mrs. Owens looked at Homer for his cue. Homer asked, "Why don't ye join us fer supper tonight?"

THE ENGAGEMENT

"Great! That would be nice, but first I have a reason for being here. Is it okay if I speak freely, sir?" Paul asked.

"Ye seem nervous. What's on your mind, young fella?" asked Homer.

"I came to Boone to learn more about Sheriff Reed for a research paper that I'm doing. When I drove into town, I saw the sign advertising cabins for rent. After I registered at the park registration office, I was assigned to Cabin 16. The attendant said, 'You will be next door to Homer Yancey a famous investigator who is here on a local high-profile murder case." He then added that he thought you were working with the Watauga County sheriff.

"That is why I am here with you right now. I would like to tell you the connection. You see, my research paper is about dishonorably discharged veterans in North Carolina. I narrowed it down to twenty-seven veterans who had died, nineteen who were World War II disabled veterans, fourteen who were currently in nursing homes, seven who are in federal prison, the whereabouts of six are unknown, five are retired and now over the age of seventy-five and seven were listed as presently in the workforce and paying federal income taxes. I have been focusing on the veterans still in the workforce and their quality of life after being dishonorably discharged. Sheriff Reed is one of those seven veterans.

"Sir, he received a dishonorable discharge from the military for what they consider the most reprehensible conduct. My inquiries revealed that this type of discharge could only have been rendered by conviction at a general court-martial for a serious offense. Sheriff Reed was convicted of sexual assault that called for a dishonorable discharge as part of the sentence.

THE ENGAGEMENT

"Mr. Yancey, I learned that those who receive a dishonorable discharge lose all of their military benefits and are forbidden from receiving or possessing firearms. Obviously, the sheriff possesses a firearm. Sir, I wanted to let you know this information and it can be verified. I have no idea what to do with the information, but thought I would seek your advice," Paul was silent but watched the surprised look on most of the investigators in the room and wondered what it meant.

"Paul, you have just become a gift from heaven," Tom said. "This information is of tremendous help to us. Anything else you can tell us about the sheriff that came up from your research?"

"I guess there is one more thing, but I'm not sure how important it is to you. I decided to see if Sheriff Reed was ever married. I learned that although he never married, he was once engaged to marry ... Sorry, just a minute. I have her name somewhere." He paused and shuffled through the papers he was holding. He was engaged to Stephanie Lynn Hicks. I learned that she married Matthew Wright and they live here in Watauga County. The timeframe of her engagement being terminated to Sheriff Allan Reed appears to be shortly after he was dishonorably discharged for sexual assault," Paul said.

This time when Paul looked around the room, he saw looks of shock on everyone's faces. "I'm sorry, have I said something wrong?" Paul asked.

Homer got up, went over to Paul, and said, "Young feller, ye are a gift from heaven. Ye git my dessert tonight! Wahoo!!!" Homer exclaimed and patted Paul on the back.

Everyone was excitedly talking at once. Homer finally yelled, "Hush up, guys. This feller jest give us a major clue and he ain't got no idea why we're so excited." Homer looked to Tom for permission to offer Paul an explanation.

Tom rose and said, "Young man, we appreciate the research you shared with us on Sheriff Reed, and we want you to know that you just helped put a major piece into the puzzle. Since we just met you tonight, we need to not only digest what you just told us, but honestly, we need to make sure you are indeed who you say you are. We are investigators and we verify everything, so please don't take offense to this."

"None taken, sir," Paul said with sincerity. "Do I still get to eat with you?" he asked.

His comment caused everyone to laugh and it relieved a tense moment. "Yes, of course," replied Tom.

During supper, Homer noticed Nick left for about twenty minutes. When MacFayden returned, he walked over to Homer and whispered to him that he had the FBI confirm Paul Castile's identity and that he was, indeed, a research student at North Carolina State University. The FBI also spoke with Paul's research instructor, Professor Chambers, who verified that Paul was researching dishonorably discharged North Carolina veterans.

Homer tapped his glass to get everyone's attention. When the talking stopped, Homer looked at Paul and said, "Paul, in our business, we have to make sure everybody is shootin' straight with us, or we could lose our case. We're working with the North Carolina FBI," and motioned to Frank and Nick, who raised their hands for Paul to see. "While we was eatin' and talkin,' Nick called the local FBI Field Office and they said ye are who ye said ye are and that ye are working on learnin' bout veterans in the state who have dishonorable discharges. Again, please don't git bent out of shape 'cause we double checked who ye are," Homer said. "We do ask that ye don't talk to the sheriff cause it could mess up our investigation. If ye do talk to him we will have to put you in jail for interfering with our investigation. Ye got it, Paul?" Homer continued. "The good news is ye still git my dessert tonight."

Everyone laughed.

After the dessert and more time getting to know everyone, Paul told them goodnight. He thanked Mrs. Owens for the supper and told her he was a starving college student and the meal hit the spot. He turned to Homer and said, "Especially Homer's piece of homemade cherry pie with ice cream," and laughed.

"Thank you, Homer for a very pleasant night. I hope I'll see you and your team again. I plan to drive back to college in two days."

Chapter 19
The Political Opponent

As Paul stepped onto the porch, Brayden and Tyler followed him. Tyler asked, "Paul would you be willing to testify in court the information you shared with us tonight about Sheriff Reed, if called on to do so?"

"Yes, it would be an honor. If you have a piece of paper and a pen, I'll write down my contact info."

Brayden reached for his small notebook in his shirt pocket with a pen attached to it. He handed it to Paul.

Paul printed his name, apartment address at NC State, and cell phone number. "I enjoyed tonight, and I hope to see y'all again soon. Goodnight, Brayden. Goodnight, Tyler." They shook hands and Paul left.

Homer motioned for Tom to step into the living room with him. "Tom, it's time fer our nightly git together in the van. Do you thank we oughta let Nick and Brian stay fer our meetin'?" "Let's wait until they leave. I want to be absolutely sure we can trust them before we divulge all we have uncovered in this investigation. What do you think, Homer?"

"I'm with ye on that."

Nick and Brian were in the kitchen thanking Mrs. Owens for the delicious meal. Brian said that since it worked for Paul, he wanted her to know that he and Nick were starving FBI agents in case there was ever any extra food. Brian gave her a pitiful expression and patted his stomach. Mrs. Owens laughed long and hard.

"I'll see what I can arrange," she told them. "It was a pleasure to meet you both. Goodnight." They both gave her a hug.

THE POLITICAL OPPONENT

"Goodnight, men. Thanks for inviting us for supper. We'll touch base with you tomorrow," Nick said. They left and Victoria stood at the window and watched them drive away.

"Okay, time fer our nightly meeting. Let's not lallygag. We done got us a lot to talk about and it's gittin' later by the minute. Come on, Duke, ye can go, too," Homer said.

Duke jumped up and ran to Homer's side and walked with him to the van. He was the first to get in the van, and after Homer sat down, Duke lay by his feet and quickly went to sleep.

"Man, this here day sure started out interestin'. Steven, bring us up to speed on what done happen," Homer said.

Steven summarized the meeting with Nick Washburn. "We think that the FBI can be of help in this investigation. Agent Washburn was quick to verify Paul Castile's identity."

Next, they talked about Paul revealing that Sheriff Reed was once engaged to Stephanie, and that he received a dishonorable discharge due to a sexual assault. The reason they didn't get married was likely due to his conviction of the horrendous sexual assault. Also discussed was the fact that because the sheriff can't possess a firearm, it probably meant that more than likely, no one knew he was dishonorably discharged, or he wouldn't have been elected sheriff.

"I appreciate everyone's silence about Stephanie when Paul said he learned she had married Matthew Wright. I really don't think he knows that it is Stephanie's murder that we are investigating and right now, I don't think we should tell him," Tom said.

"We need to make sure we've got all the 't's' crossed and the 'i's' dotted to make sure it's sewed up tight when we give all this stuff to the lawyers. No ifs, and's, or but's about it. We need to have an airtight case against the sheriff," Homer said.

Zach spoke up, "Homer? There is something I would like to know. What is the connection between the murder of Stephanie Wright and the attempted murder of my dear wife?"

"Good question, Zach. I'm thinkin' that bullet was meant fer me and Victoria just got in the way. We don't rightly know who pulled the trigger. At Yancey Investigative Services we don't assume anything, so we can't assume the bullet was for me. We do need an answer to your question, Zach. We'll work on that," Homer promised.

"When will we hear from internal affairs regarding Bill Carpenter's alleged fabricating of evidence?" asked Tyler.

"Steven would ye mind finding out fer us and let us know somethang as soon as ye know?" asked Homer.

"I think we're done fer now. Good job, guys. See ye at 7:00 a.m. fer breakfast. Let's get some shuteye," Homer instructed.

Everyone exited the van and headed to their rooms. "Night, Steven. Call me in the morning," Homer said as Steven walked towards his car. Homer walked Duke then went inside. While Homer was turning out the lights, Brayden came into the living room.

"I meant to add that we need to see if we can find out what Stephanie wrote on the last page of her logbook. It may not be words that are pertinent to anything regarding our investigation. However, it might be information that is valuable. What are your thoughts, Homer?" asked Brayden.

"Brayden, you're right and we need to git on that real quick. Let's get Zach and Amelia to chase that rabbit," Homer commented. "If that's alright with you."

"Yes! Let's turn over every rock, as they say," said Brayden.

"Would you tell Zach and Amelia to meet with me in the mornin' 'bout quarter till seven?" asked Homer.

"I'd be glad to, Homer. I'll just call them from my room tonight and tell them. Goodnight, Homer," Brayden said. The two men walked down the hall to their rooms.

The next morning, Amelia and Zach were both prompt for their meeting with Homer. They were already in the living room sipping their coffee when Homer and Duke arrived. Homer told them he would be right back after he took Duke for a brief walk.

Once Homer came back inside, Zach asked, "Have we done something wrong, Homer?"

"Of course not. Relax. I jest wanna give y'all an assignment. Let's go to the dining room so ye can spread your notebooks out," Homer instructed. When Tom came into the living room, Homer invited him to be part of the meeting he was having with Zach and Amelia.

"I want the two of ye to figger out what Stephanie wrote on the last page of her logbook before she tore it out. I want ye to work together on this," Homer instructed.

"Zach, why don't we use the forensic document examination method," Amelia suggested.

"What is that?" asked Homer.

"It's just a fancy way of saying that we use science in analyzing the document," she answered. "The indented impressions in the paper beneath the sheet that was torn out can be revealed by using an oblique high intensity light. I think this method is what we should use first, don't you agree, Zach?"

"Yes! Great idea, Amelia. I've read about that method but have never used it. Have you?" Zach commented as he sipped more coffee.

"No, but in this case, I think it would be very useful.

I have two questions. Where do we find the logbook?" she asked. "Also, where can we go to get an oblique high intensity light?"

"There is a place in Boone where we can get one, but it's going to cost a few hundred dollars." Zach said.

"Don't give that a second thought, Zach," Homer said.

"I'm ready to go if you are," Amelia said.

"Maybe we should wait until after breakfast and that way even the stores will be open," Zach said with a laugh.

After breakfast, they drove into Boone and Zach found the store where they were able to buy the light they needed. Once it was purchased, they went to Hickory Grove Baptist Church to get the logbook.

THE POLITICAL OPPONENT

Zach slapped his head and said, "Homer, Tom, and I put the logbook in a labeled evidence bag and took it to the sheriff's office. We will need to go there and hopefully they will let us either check it out or photograph a few pages. Just as they were about to walk out of Stephanie's office, the janitor walked in.

"Oh, excuse me. I was just going to clean Mrs. Stephanie's office. I can come back another time."

"We were just leaving. I'm Zach Thomas and this is Amelia Davis. We are attorneys with Yancey Investigative Services. What is your name, sir?"

"Lee Vogel."

"It's nice to meet you, Mr. Vogel. Maybe we'll see each other again. Have a nice day," Amelia said.

"You, too," he said.

Amelia and Zach went straight to the sheriff's office. They were pleased, yet surprised that they were allowed to check out the book.

Once back at the cabin, Homer came into the dining room as Amelia and Zach were setting up the equipment on the dining room table. When they turned on the oblique light, the words started popping up on the previously empty page.

"What does it say, Zach?" asked Brayden.

"It says that Brayden is going to give Zach his dessert for the rest of the month," Zach said.

"Oh, stop it," Amelia said.

"It does say that Stephanie is trying to convince her brother, Robert, to run against Allan for sheriff. This time, I'm not kidding. She said that she needs to tell Robert all about Allan's secret, because when it gets out, Allan will be ruined," Zach said.

"It sounds like we need to pay Robert a visit and see if Stephanie talked to him about the sheriff. If she did tell him about the dishonorable discharge, why ain't we heard from him?" Homer asked.

"Zach, find out when the sheriff's reelection bid is and if Robert Hicks qualified to run against him," Homer said with urgency in his voice. "Oh, and another thing, find out Mr. Hicks' address. We may need to pay him a visit."

"I'm on it, boss!" Zach said. He told Amelia he was going to get his computer and that he would be right back.

Zach returned within minutes and booted his computer. While that was happening, he said to Amelia, "All of the cases that Yancey Investigative Services has solved are on my computer. They are filed by the name of the deceased. For me, that is the easiest way to find the case. So, you need to have your own method regarding cases.

"This case is under 'Stephanie Wright,'" he told her.

"Thanks, Zach. I like the way you have organized it. Do you mind if I just use your method? That way, if you need something off of my computer, it will be easily found," she suggested.

"Of course, I don't mind. You are welcome to look at my computer anytime. There is nothing on it that is of personal nature. I have another computer at home that I use for that purpose," Zach said with a grin.

THE POLITICAL OPPONENT

"Let's see if we can find out when the primary is scheduled, or if it has already occurred. We can see if there is a sample ballot online and if so, we should be able to see the sheriff's name and his opponent's name."

"I am learning a lot, Zach. Thank you for taking the time to teach me even the little details. Do you mind showing me how to research the election stuff?" she asked.

"Sure. First, I go online and search qualifications and deadlines for sheriff of Watauga County. We will be directed to a site that will tell us when the Democratic and Republican primaries are scheduled. Did you know that they are not held on the same day? This website should also tell us the names of the Republican and Democratic candidates.

"Since I will now know which party Sheriff Allan Reed is affiliated with, I'll use google to get his home address." Amelia said.

"Yes. That would be the quickest way. Another option would be to call the County Democratic Party and tell them we are working with the FBI on a high-profile murder case and need a copy of the Sheriff's home address. Tell him he can either give us the address over the phone or we can send two of our agents to pick up a copy." Zach explained.

"Why don't we do this now? Homer did say he wanted the information quickly," Amelia reminded him.

The two lawyers started the process to get a copy of the sheriff's qualifying papers. After ten minutes of research, they found that Allan Joseph Reed filed qualifying papers with the Watauga County Republican

Party. Currently, he is the only Republican candidate for the office of Watauga County sheriff.

Zach and Amelia then searched to see if the sheriff had opposition in the election. The Watauga County Democratic Party website posted a list of candidates in the upcoming primary. Robert Nathanial Hicks was listed as the only qualifying Democratic candidate for the office of sheriff.

"Okay, we have it! Now, let's give a copy to the boss. I think he went back outside, " Zach instructed.

"We didn't find out the dates of the primaries. I think we should have answers ready in case he asks, and if he doesn't ask, then we will look good because we anticipated his question. Don't you agree?" asked Amelia.

"Wow! You are brilliant! Thanks for saving my hide, Amelia," Zach said with a grin. "Okay, back to the computer. I think all we have to do is ask when the election will be held for Watauga County sheriff." Zach typed in the question. "Okay, it says that the Republican primary will be held in four months. The Democratic primary will be held a month later." Zach said, then asked, "Are we ready to report to Homer now?"

"Yes, let's find him."

Homer and Duke were on the front porch. It was a beautiful day with a slight breeze and Homer was in a comfortable porch chair making sounds like a small outboard motor.

"I hate to wake him, but he said this was important. I guess it's necessary," Zach said as he slowly walked over to Homer. Duke stood and looked straight at Zach as though he was wondering what Zach had in mind.

"It's okay, Duke. Good boy," Zach said as he was rethinking whether he should wake his boss.

Amelia said, "Homer! Wake up, sir!" Duke walked over to where Amelia was standing and licked her hand. Homer was awake.

Zach shot a disapproving expression towards Amelia. She just shrugged her shoulders in innocence.

"Homer, we have a report on the election for sheriff of Watauga County," Amelia said with a smile.

"Let's have it," Homer said.

Chapter 20
The Withdrawal

Homer was pleased with their report and what they found out about Robert Hicks.

"I reckon we need to go see Mr. Hicks. Zach, call the guy and set it up, and tell him me and Tom wanna see him. Now don't go pitchin' a duck fit. It ain't that I don't want ye 'round, I jest don't want a lot of people showin' up and makin' him uncomfortable. Tom knows how to ask good questions, and y'all tell me all the time that I can tell when somebody ain't shootin' straight with us."

"Don't worry about it, Homer. We aren't that sensitive. Besides, lawyers aren't investigators, but we do enjoy research. Thanks for letting us examine the facts so you can be equipped for your meeting," said Zach.

"Let me know when ye got the meetin' set up. Ye can just tell the guy we got a few questions 'bout the day

Stephanie was killed and we are hopin' he might help us," Homer suggested.

Amelia was so excited that Homer was using them that she asked Zach if she could set up the meeting with Mr. Hicks.

"Of course, Amelia. You are as much a part of this team as I am. Do you want me to be near when you place the call?" he asked.

"Would you, please? You can have my dessert tonight," she said with a smile.

"Well, then, by all means, call!" Zach said.

Amelia placed the call. "Mr. Hicks, this is Amelia Davis with Yancey Investigative Services. We are investigating the murder of your sister, Stephanie. As her brother, you probably know her better than anyone else.

There are a few questions we thought you might be able to answer. We would appreciate it if you could meet us in the morning at 7:00 a.m. at the coffee shop on Sherman Street. Would you be willing to meet briefly with us?"

"Yes, of course. I really miss Stephanie and if I can be of help with your investigation, I'll give you all the time you need. I'll see you at the coffee shop in the morning," said Mr. Hicks.

The next morning, Tom, Homer, and Steven introduced themselves to Robert Hicks. After introductions and placing coffee orders, they sat at a table in the back.

Tom started the conversation, "Mr. Hicks, allow me to start. Were you close to your sister?"

"We were the only children born to our parents and we were only seventeen months apart. As young people, we did everything together. I was a football player and Stephanie was a cheerleader, so we ran with the same crowd. If I didn't have a date or Stephanie didn't have one, we did something together. So, yes, we were close," replied Robert.

"Did she tell ye her secrets?" asked Homer.

"Secrets. Hum. I'll have to think on that one." His eyes narrowed. "Tell me what you are referring to and if I know anything about it, I'll gladly tell you," Robert suggested as he folded his arms.

"Were you aware that Stephanie and Sheriff Reed were engaged years ago and that she broke it off after he was dishonorably discharged from the military?" asked Tom.

THE WITHDRAWAL

"Wow! I didn't see that one coming. Yes, I was aware of their romance. He broke her heart," Robert informed the team. "What does that have to do with me?"

"Robert, we believe that Stephanie asked you to run against Sheriff Reed. We think she wanted to punish him by exposing the fact that he was dishonorably discharged and legally may not posses a weapon. Robert, do you have any law enforcement experience? Do you really want to be the sheriff of Watauga County or are you doing this for your little sister?" asked Tom.

"I've been following the investigation, and everyone says that Yancey Investigative Services are the very best team to find Stephanie's murderer. After the amazing research that you just presented, I'll have to agree that you are indeed the best," Robert said.

"Thank you, Robert. We think this is the killer's motive. We believe he wanted Stephanie out of the picture before the election, because if his secret were to be made public and leaked to the media, he would be finished politically," Tom related.

"We need somethang from you, Robert. We think we know what happened, but we need ye to tell us, so we'll know if we done got it right. Now don't git me wrong, Robert, we ain't on nobody's side, especially the sheriff. It's our job to git the truth. That thar's why we done got ye to meet with us today. We gotta confirm our theory 'bout the motive fer her murder," Homer said. "So, what's it gonna be, Robert? Do ye want the truth to be known and help us catch a murderer or do ye want to run fer somethang we thank ye don't even want. Do ye really want to be sheriff, Robert?"

THE WITHDRAWAL

"No, not really. I did it for Stephanie. Your theory is correct," Robert said remorsefully. "You guys really play hardball, but I do appreciate your diligence in finding Stephanie's killer."

Steven asked, "Would you be willing to provide testimony in court as to what you just told us, if asked to do so?"

"Without question. I'll help anyway you deem appropriate," Robert promised. When he stood to leave, he said that he had an errand to run. "I'm going to withdraw from the sheriff's race. Maybe I can get a good night's sleep after I do that," he said smiling. "It was nice to meet you gentlemen. If you need me for anything else, please don't hesitate to call me." Robert shook hands with everyone and then Tom, Homer, and Steven left.

"Steven, what happens if the sheriff goes to prison and Robert has dropped out of the race? How will the next sheriff be determined?" asked Tom.

"The Governor will appoint a sheriff. Don't look at me, I'm not interested! I'm changing jobs and moving into a bunkhouse in Alabama," Steven said with a wide grin. Homer and Tom started clapping.

Meanwhile, the sheriff was sitting at his desk wondering if he had covered himself on all sides.

"*Is there any evidence I accidentally left behind or is there anyone who knows what I did?* he asked himself while staring out his office window. "*It sure looks like Homer Yancey's team is getting close to winding this case up, and I don't want my name to be at the top of their short list,*" he said as he stood and started pacing his office. "*If someone did see me, who would it have been? Or, if *someone overheard me talk to her or about her, who would it have been?"* As he continued pacing, he said, *"Think, Allan, think."*

He left his office briefly, just long enough to go to the vending machine for a soft drink. When he came back in his office, he dropped his soft drink, and the spilled drink made a big mess on the floor.

"That's just what I need, a mess on the floor the day before our new janitor starts to work here. Janitor! That's it! I haven't even considered the fact that Lee Vogel may have been cleaning the church that day. If he was at the church, did he see or hear anything? Why haven't I thought of him before now?" the sheriff asked himself.

"Lee is such a quiet man. If he did see or hear something, I seriously doubt that he has told anyone. If I can verify that he was a witness, then all I need to do is

threaten him and I believe he will be so scared that he won't squeal on me! I think I may pay the guy a visit," the sheriff decided.

Just as he was about to leave his office, his phone rang.

"Allan, this is Robert. I've decided I'm not really interested in being sheriff. Stephanie begged me to run against you, so I did," Robert confessed. "Allan, let's cut to the chase, 'the cat is out of the bag.' Robert reluctantly continued. "Not only that, but you know, Allan, that I know that you know that I know what you did. And because I know that you know, you know "you need to fish or cut bait." Robert explained. "Allan, it's over. It's time to 'face the music,'" Robert said. He was hoping that Allan was truly listening to his advice. "Allan, are you still there? Hello? Allan?"

THE WITHDRAWAL

There was no response on the other end of the phone because Sheriff Reed had stopped listening and was getting inside his county sheriff's vehicle. After talking to Robert, the reality of serving life in prison was consuming the sheriff's thoughts. There was no doubt in his mind that Lee Vogel squealed on him.

Before he went to Hickory Grove Baptist Church, Sheriff Reed stopped at his bank and used the ATM to withdraw all his money in checking and savings. He then used four credit cards to get cash advances. Thinking like criminals he had arrested over the years, he then filled the county vehicle. While he was at the drug store buying four disposable urinals, he called Chick-Fil-A and ordered ten Number One's with bottled waters. He told them that the order was to go. He gave them his county credit card number and told them he would be there in ten minutes.

All set, he drove to the church. There were no cars in the parking lot. Sheriff Reed went inside and finally located Lee in the Men's Sunday School classroom.

"Lee! It's Sheriff Reed. I know you are in there. Come out," the sheriff shouted.

Lee humbly complied. "What do you want, Allan?" he said trembling.

"I want the truth, Lee. Did you see or hear anything the night that Stephanie Wright was murdered? Were you here at the church?" asked Sheriff Reed.

"At first, Allan, all I saw was a man come in with a head covering, shoes, gloves, and a mask. I really didn't know who it was or what they were up to, so I hid in the broom closet," replied Lee. "But I recognized your voice when you were threatening Mrs. Wright and I got really scared.

"I watched with the broom closet with the door slightly opened. I saw you drag a large leaf bag out the door. I assumed it was Mrs. Wright because I didn't hear her scream or talk anymore.

"I swear, Allan, I ain't told nobody nothing! I swear," Lee said as the sheriff walked closer and closer to him.

"Lee, if I hear anything about you talking to that Homer guy, then your daughter, Mary, will be locked up again and good luck on trying to bond her out!"

The next thing Lee remembered was waking up on the floor. He was bleeding from his nose and it felt like he had been punched in the gut. The sheriff was gone. Lee reached for his cell phone.

"Is this Mr. Yancey?" Lee asked.

"Yep, this is Homer."

"Mr. Yancey," Lee began.

"Ye can call me Homer."

"Homer, this is Lee Vogel. Would it be possible for you to come to the church as soon as possible?"

"We'll be thar in a flash," Homer replied and ended the call. "Tom, Duke, come with me. NOW." Homer said with urgency, and they headed out the door.

When they arrived at the church, Lee met them at the back door.

THE WITHDRAWAL

"Man, you need medical attention! I'm calling 911," Homer said and then told Duke to SEARCH. Duke started sniffing and searching throughout the church building. He came back to Homer and sat down. "Good boy, Duke," Homer said as he patted his dog's head.

Lee was sitting in a chair when the paramedics arrived. Pastor White came in the back door to see what all the commotion was about. When he saw Lee, he nearly cried.

Lee was treated and told that he did not need to be transported to the hospital but recommended that he make an appointment with his doctor tomorrow.

When the paramedics left, Lee told Homer, Tom and Pastor White what happened when Sheriff Reed paid him a visit. Just as he finished talking about the Sheriff,

Homer's phone rang. He wouldn't have answered it except he noticed it was from Robert Hicks.

"This is Homer."

"Homer, this is Robert Hicks. I am calling to tell you about the phone conversation that I had earlier with Allan Reed. I told him that 'he's like a rock only dumber,' if he thinks he's not going to be caught. That's when I told him he needs to get a lawyer. Homer, I believe instead of staying to fight this, he is going to flee. He may be gone already."

"Thanks, Robert. We're on it," Homer hung up and immediately called FBI Agent Nick Washburn and told him the situation.

"Homer, I will meet you, Steven, and Tom at your cabin in fifteen minutes or less. Pack a few clothes. We could be gone a few days. You are the lead detective in this case and I'm keeping my promise that we'll not take it away from you. If he flees across the state line, I'll have authority, but I want you along so monitor the sheriff's whereabouts," Agent Washburn instructed, then ended the call.

Once Sheriff Reed had gathered his supplies and paid a visit to Lee, he got in his new county vehicle. It was a Ford Police Interceptor Utility vehicle. He thought to himself, *"I'm sure glad I've got this car. It has all the bells and whistles I can use in case there is a standoff. It has adequate space for sleeping, for mounted weapons, and for emergency equipment in the event I get wounded."*

He turned on the blue lights and drove through town as though on official business.

He was aware that once he left Watauga County his vehicle would blend in with other official law enforcement cars. Most people probably wouldn't notice the signage on his vehicle, "Sheriff Watauga County".

Because he had no indication he was being followed, he used this to his advantage and set his GPS for his Uncle Eugene's ranch in Boise, Idaho. It would be a long trip, but he knew he would be welcomed there, no questions asked.

Allan had made this trip several times. He occasionally used back roads which he knew would make it harder to locate him. He drove fast, but at a steady speed. By noon, he was in Ohio, and by nightfall, he was somewhere in Indiana.

THE WITHDRAWAL

Meanwhile, in the FBI's black van, Homer, Tom, and Steven were intrigued with the equipment that was installed for their use.

"Nick, thanks for bringing us along. Sitting here in the backseat, we are drooling over the impressive capabilities available to you in this vehicle. Do you have an extra car like this?" asked Tom. The men laughed.

After telling Homer, Steven, and Tom about the van's capabilities, Agent Washburn informed them that he had issued a nationwide BOLO (Be On the Look Out). Within minutes, he was notified that the sheriff was in Indiana.

Agent Washburn was granted authority by the FBI Field Office in North Carolina to call on the local Indiana FBI for assistance.

He then called and briefly explained the situation to the Agent in Charge, Tom McBrayer. Agent Washburn requested that two armed helicopters follow the sheriff and hover at a surveilling distance until Agents MacFayden and Washburn arrived. McBrayer gave his approval and said his men would be alert and ready.

Tom, Homer, Steven and the two agents made few stops during the night as they traveled to Indiana to arrest Allan Reed for murder. Early the next morning, Agent Washburn was told by one of the helicopter pilots that the sheriff spent the night next to the Whitewater River in Indiana.

"Thank you for keeping us updated. Has he left yet?" asked Agent MacFayden.

"No sir," replied the pilot.

"Notify me if he attempts to leave the area," Agent Washburn instructed. "We are approximately fifty miles from you. Would you please send me his exact location?"

"Roger that, sir."

The black van carrying Agent Washburn, Agent MacFayden, Homer, Steven, and Tom, arrived and parked a short distance away from the sheriff's parked car.

Agent MacFayden had been operating the equipment inside the van. He told Agent Washburn that Special Agent-in-Charge Tom McBrayer was waiting for instructions. Agent Washburn was handed a microphone.

"Good morning, sir. Once again, we appreciate your cooperation and assistance. We will be on location in approximately ten minutes. Can your agents hear my voice?" asked Agent Washburn.

"Yes, sir. They are awaiting your orders," replied Agent McBrayer.

"I want every agent to approach the scene as silently as possible. Position yourself with your weapon ready. When you are given my signal, point your weapon towards the man in the sheriff's uniform. We are working on a diversion to get him outside his vehicle. We are hopeful that the police helicopter will hover above him. When you see the helicopter, please let there be total silence on your part. However, I want you to stand facing our suspect and point your gun towards him. Do not fire unless instructed! Thank you." Agent Washburn told everyone.

The black van moved closer as Agent Washburn instructed both helicopters to hover low above the sheriff's car. "At my cue, point your weapon at the sheriff and using

THE WITHDRAWAL

your loudspeaker, order him to drop his weapon. While we are moving in from behind, keep him engaged so he will be focused on what you guys are doing. We are hoping he will point his weapon towards you. When this happens, let it play out as we discussed on the phone. Thank you for your help in capturing this murderer," Agent Washburn said.

It did play out just as planned. Both FBI helicopters hovered above Sheriff Reed's car which muffled other sounds. The agents in the helicopters pointed their guns at him and used loudspeakers to order him to exit the vehicle and surrender.

Allan knew he would face life in prison if he surrendered. He would rather die first. When Sheriff Reed got out of his car, he aimed his AR15 at the first chopper's blades.

Someone tapped Allan on his shoulder and shouted to be heard above the helicopter noise, "I wouldn't do that if I were you, **Allan**." When the sheriff turned to see who was talking to him, he not only saw that it was Homer, but just behind him were at least **twenty-five** FBI agents in full tactical gear with their weapons pointed straight at him.

As instructed earlier by Agent Washburn, Homer jumped out of the way and Watauga County Chief Deputy Sheriff Steven Adamson, Agents Washburn and MacFayden ran up to Allan, secured his weapon and placed him in handcuffs. Allan did not resist.

Chief Deputy Sheriff Adamson said, "Mr. Reed, you are under arrest for the murder of Stephanie Lynn Hicks. We are going to transport you to the Watauga County Sheriff's Department, in Boone, North Carolina."

THE WITHDRAWAL

Allan was led by several heavily armed agents to the car driven by FBI Agent David Simmons, the local Assistant FBI Agent-in-Charge. Allan knew his fate, but at the same time admired Homer's investigative skills. He made eye contact with Homer, acknowledged him with a smirk, then kept his eyes to the ground as he shuffled to the car.

THE END

Epilogue

Sheriff Allan Reed was apprehended in Indiana. In compliance with federal law, North Carolina Governor Robert Burns requested of Indiana Governor Ron Rutledge to extradite Allan Reed to the authorities in Boone, North Carolina.

During the prosecutor's powerful examination of evidence with Mr. Reed prior to his trial, she was able to obtain his confession regarding the attempted murder of Victoria Thomas. The prosecutor determined that Mrs. Wright's death met the requirements for first degree murder. In addition, Mr. Reed was also charged with the attempted murder of Victoria Thomas, fabricating evidence, and obstruction of justice.

Allan Reed's trial was held in Federal Court in Butner, North Carolina. He was found guilty on all counts and is currently serving a life sentence without parole at the

Federal Correctional Institution Rivers in Hertford County, North Carolina.

Deputy Bill Carpenter was found guilty by Watauga County Sheriff's Department's Internal Affairs and was arrested on charges of fabricating evidence and obstructing justice. He was found guilty on both counts by a jury of his peers in Watauga County District Court. Mr. Carpenter is currently serving a five-year prison term in Central Prison for Men in Raleigh, North Carolina.

The charges were dropped against **Mr. Matthew Wright**, and he was released from the Watauga County Jail. Three years after the death of his wife, Stephanie, Matthew was offered the Superintendent of Education position for the Boone City Board of Education. His new wife, Melanie, attended the Board meeting announcing his promotion.

Chief Deputy Sheriff Steven Adamson assumed the position of Sheriff of Watauga County for six months after the arrest of Allan Reed. He then relocated to Oneonta, Alabama, where he became a detective with Yancey Investigative Services. Steven is currently enjoying his new home in the bunkhouse.

Yancey Investigative Services team members and their leader, Homer Yancey solved Stephanie Wright's murder case. The murderer is currently serving a life sentence for his horrific crime. After the trial, the team stayed another week in Boone. Homer had promised the team a week of fun together as an escape from detective work. They slept late and played on the Watauga River. Homer rented water scooters, canoes, kayaks, and a large sailboat. They ate out nearly every meal and watched movies in the evening. When it was time to head back to Alabama, Homer gave up his seat on the airplane, left a day before the team and rode back home with Zach, Victoria, and Duke.

The team is currently working on a high-profile, top secret, classified case.

About the Author, Judi McGuire
By: Homer Yancey

I believe Judi McGuire invented the helicopter, the electric light, and the internal combustion engine. Rumors suggest that she was friends of Alexander Graham Bell when he was testing his first telephone system. Judi was also the first person to climb Mt. McKinley. She has flown to the Space Station and back in one day and has written two thousand highly regarded novels.

Judi is also a great teller of stories — but not all of them are true, for instance, the one you hold in your hand.

Homer Yancey

Please visit her website, www.AlabamaAuthor.com for clues, characters, and contact information.

Email: judi.alabamaauthor@gmail.com

Judi McGuire
Alabama Author

Writing has been a passion for Judi. However, like most women, her role as wife, mother of two daughters, and a demanding full-time career, momentarily put on hold her dream of authoring a novel. As Alabama PTA State President, Judi's determination as an advocate for children didn't go unnoticed. Her tireless work in Washington, D.C. was rewarded by an appointment to serve in an Alabama Congressman's administration. Within a few years, Alabama Governor Guy Hunt honored her with an appointment in his Cabinet as Education Advisor. After leaving the governor's office, she served as Governmental Relations Officer for the largest healthcare organization in Alabama. Judi's lobbying career spanned over thirty years.

When traveling to Washington, D.C., or Montgomery, Alabama, Judi would read fiction murder mystery books to unwind after reading large pieces of legislation. Judi has now set aside the law books and picked up a pen to author her own stories. As a murder mystery writer, it's Judi's goal to author compelling stories that will draw readers into the mysteries and transform them into detectives who will uncover clues and discover 'whodunit' on their own.

Once their daughters left the nest, Judi and her husband, Tim built a home in Blount County. Inspired by the charm, history, and beauty of her new surroundings, Judi became a successful Alabama author. Judi's career experience and knowledge have helped her develop page-turning writing techniques and a unique literary style fans love.

In Loving Memory
Robert Eugene Seals
(Homer)
12/26/51 – 04/29/22